Esc-Ape: A Journey

A novel
by
Alan Milligan

Produced by Alan Milligan
alanmilligan56@yahoo.co.uk

This story is dedicated to my daughter, Angela. She was about ten or eleven at the time of writing, now by the time of publication she is all grown up and married, but still my wee girl.

Angie.

X

ESC-APE: A JOURNEY

Chapter 1

Blair Drummond Safari Park, Stirling, Scotland

A car rolls slowly into the monkey enclosure, with the young family inside, all peering around in eager anticipation.

"Stop the car Dad!" the youngest one urged in a whispered roar, "There's one sitting beside the road!"

On coming to a halt its entire occupancy moved over to the left hand side of the vehicle.

"She's got a baby!" exclaimed her older sister, "It's holding on upside down!"

The youngest one went to put down the window.

Forgetting.

Her Dad soon reminded her, checking around as he spoke. "Keep the windows up kids, remember they're wild animals, they could give you a nasty scratch, and maybe even bite you if you're not careful"

His words of warning had little or no effect on his wife and children, they "Ahhhhd!" in perfect unison as they peered outside the car to the little monkey sitting in a broken clump of rye-grass, not ten feet from the parked vehicle.

"The baby's so sweet!"

"It's gorgeous!!"

The young family stared animatedly onward in the direction of the mother Rhesus and its infant.

Even the Father, hopeless in intrigue, watched

helplessly on.

Slowly erecting herself, the female macaque paced to the front of the car, and as the family's eye's followed her as one, she moved out of their sight to sit just under the registration plate. Discovering a discarded peanut by the side of the road, she munched at the morsel quickly.

The children were now quite excitable worrying about the car moving over the monkeys, they advised their father immediately.

"DON'T MOVE THE CAR DAD!"

He smiled reassuringly, whispering quietly to his wife.

"Don't want to flatten the little guys"...

He rested his foot firmly on the brakes, murmuring in mock-tones.

"We'll never get out of here today!"

Shaking her head knowingly, his wife smiled back to him.

The five occupants of the car stared dead ahead, chins raised as high as was possible, each one trying to catch sight of the monkey and its clinging infant.

With baited breath and holding onto their mum and dad's shoulders, the children willed the Rhesus to re-appear into their anxious view.

Then as if to answer their thoughts, the mother Rhesus leapt from the path, and in one seasoned, practised movement, she was sitting, rested on the bonnet of their car. Still the baby gripped tightly underneath as the two adults and three children watched helplessly on, each one almost hypnotised by the wonderful, almost magical sight before them.

A wild Rhesus Macaque and suckling infant, sitting on the bonnet of their car, and displayed as if in a wonderful wildlife television programme.

BUT NOW, RIGHT IN FRONT OF THEM.

Yes, this was real life, and the beasts were no further away than a few feet from them.

Almost touching, patting distance, which each of the kids desperately wanted to do; no matter how much their father had earlier warned them.

By this point the children had almost stopped breathing, such was their fascination.

Mandy whispered into her dad's ear as she clung around his neck, standing behind him, "Do you think they can see us?" she gripped tightly around his collar, "Like, through the windscreen?"

Cause it looked as though they didn't

Dad nodded back.

"Think so...

Her older sister thought out loud, "I'd love to hold the baby, it's so beautiful!"

Even their twelve-year-old, and normally harder to please brother, smiled happily on, such was the scene of utter bliss.

The Macaque looked away from the car interior and casually lifted her top lip.

She then opened and closed her left hand twice.

As she did this, a larger male Rhesus and smaller female leapt from behind the car, and in a flash of brown fur, both were underneath it.

Then in a frenzy of great activity they set to work, completely unnoticed by the humans above.

Todo clenched the metal nuts tightly and snugly in his great jaws and released the torqued up bolts from their mounts. When released, Nnp unscrewed them quickly, her body whizzing crazily, upside down, in a manic, circular motion, underneath the car.

Her teeth clung to the bolts as she released them and freed them from their mounts.

Another four monkeys joined them and gathered around the tow-bar till it was freed. Then they mobbed the metal fixing and ran from the car as a group, completely obscuring the tow-bar from the vehicle's smiling, but blissfully ignorant occupants.

The whole operation?

It took no more than fifty seconds, with both animals working as quickly as any machine in a pit stop at a Grand-Prix race.

Quicker than any garage, or Quick-Fit fitter

By now Maya had made her way to the top of the car and watched as her team of trained, thieving simians, now huddled around the tow-bar, ran as a group toward the huts which housed them in the Safari Park.

Each of the kids below almost screamed in sheer delight as they stretched to see the monkey pad around the roof of their car.

It was so close!!

Outwardly, the Macaque seemed disinterested as it stared toward its mates, and just as she was climbing from the roof, out of sight of the family, she leaned down and nipped off the rear screen wash-wipe font, a little plastic moulding no bigger than a few centimetres square and sat with it gripped firmly in her front teeth.

Maya noticed a half-erected aerial as she started to clamber off the vehicle. There was no time for that now and it irked her somewhat as she passed it by.

Knowing that one of the other clans would release it

further down the line the simian leaned over and bent the aerial in half, annoyed at the thought of it.

As she came off the car, the larger Macaque, Todo, stood waiting for her, the clan leader, to join him.

At least five inches bigger than her, Todo was a giant of a Rhesus. Strongly built, his legs and forearms were visibly longer and more muscular than any of the other clan members, but it was his neck and shoulder muscles which stood out, almost freakishly, giving him the almost unbelievable appearance of a weightlifting monkey. He was a magnificent specimen, and just approaching his prime.

A Schwarzenegger of simians

He smiled to Maya as she lumbered back from the car, and as his lips were cleared, the hexagonal shape of a half-inch bolt head was clearly displayed in his front upper and lower teeth. The thick, heavy teeth were closed, displaying the incredible, unbelievable sight of a torque wrenched mouth.

He grinned gawkily to her as she approached.

Then they both ran to the huts, following the leading group.

A small group of Macaques stood in a circle around a little pile of various motorcar parts and fixings. They turned and smiled nervously as Maya entered the hut, followed by Todo.

She walked into the space in the gathering that was cleared for her.

"Favoured One"...

"Your Goodness"...

One by one they peeled off and stood aside, heads bowed as they sought her approval, then stood in sullen quietness, one or two upon their hind legs, awaiting her judgement.

She looked upon the pile of parts.

The heavy under-tail thing (the tow-bar).

She nodded as she pulled it away.

Side, round things (wheel trims); clutching three fingers she counted them.

Front-back things (registration plates)

The macaque closed her hand, and then held out her index finger as she counted the six.

Holding up two aerials, she nodded twice at the clean cuts on the thin cable.

Young Chee stood at the front in the line of anxious simians, him also awaiting her approval.

Maya nodded gently toward him and could tell it was his work, good, sharp teeth.

The kid done a good job.

The clan done a good job!

She raised her head to speak; the clan raised their eyebrows in anticipation.

"WE HAVE WORKED WELL THIS DAY...HE WILL BE PLEASED..."

The clan approached, relieved now and eager to hear her commendations.

"HAR-REE WILL BE HAPPY, HE WILL FEED US WELL TONIGHT!"...

The pack advanced, each one waiting to greet, to exalt her.

It was customary for the clan members to greet their leader, embracing firstly, then it was a great honour to be allowed to preen her, but not for too long, it was a token preening only.

They stood in a wilful queue, each one in their place in

the line of mixed males and females, working down in age, size and stature, down to the youngest of the cubs, one of which was her oldest son, a Chee Macaque.

As usual, Jodo, the lead male suitor, was at the head of the queue.

The most handsome, but also the vainest monkey in the whole park, he brushed the smaller and younger male and female monkeys aside. He was devilishly good looking, but arrogant and haughty, too caught up in his own appearance and sense of self-importance for Maya to really take seriously.

He had once almost caused uproar by hiding and trying to keep a self-image (wing mirror) to himself, instead of offering it to Har-ree.

She stood, as usual drawn in silence, as he greeted her.

"A fine haul your goodness, I am pleased beyond words that the clan have contented you!"...

Nodding slab-faced as he gave her a perfunctory examination. Maya wouldn't return his eager gaze. She only looked for her son in the maze of fawning simians.

"That will do Jodo"...

He backed off, touching his head as he bowed.

The preening ritual was a very natural bonding process, and every monkey was allowed to inspect the leader. This was the only time that any of the animals, younger or older, bigger or smaller, were allowed to act in any kind of fashion which may have resembled dominance.

Individually, and only for a few brief moments sometimes, the other monkeys were allowed to lift Mayas limbs, head and torso and she would comply as the grooming took place.

Some older females would talk during the grooming,

flicking her limbs up and down as the searched intently for bugs, and the males would compliment her, so much so, she was heartily bored with their company at the best of times.

And now, even her baby, the little Berra, had started to copy its elders, and would join in with whoever groomed his mother at the time.

The members of the clans of macaques had no individual names, but titles, or named positions in the clan.

The youngest member was the Berra; baby, little one, innocent and unknowing, dependant.

Next stage was the Nnp; male or female monkeys from roughly three or four months old, depending on individual development. There were a lot of invaluable tasks perfectly suited to the nimble fingers, tongue and lips, the sharp teeth and claws of the Nnp monkey, the first working stage.

Next, the almost fully-grown male and female monkeys were known as the Chee, the mainstay of the group.

Always the most conscientious, steadfastly strong and uncomplaining, these were almost the elite of the family.

Koth; fully grown males, mature and wise, but everyone knew them to be a little too worldly wise at times, not lazy, sometimes just a little slower and more selective in the tasks they performed.

Chaar; fully grown females with pretty much the same attitude as the Koth.

Craa; females carrying or nursing Berra.

Todo; a coveted and much respected position, strongest male of any, but not necessarily the most intelligent. Still, there was much food and respect with this title.

Jodo; lead male suitor and usually the Adonis, and smartest monkey.

All the above were subjects of the leader and showed untold loyalty and meek subservience to the title only held by the lead, matriarch monkey.

The Maya; dominant, strong in mind and body, her wisdom would only be questioned by another female with covetous eyes on the lead position, but the Maya was rarely challenged at this point, in the clan's daily life.

The monkeys started to call and hoot, becoming excitable when they could hear the trucks out and starting to feed the animals in their different ranges. There were three clans of macaques, their very different families who now vied with each other to see who could offer the best to their master, the human keeper, Har-ree.

The little beasts faces became set in concentrated gazes, envisaging their master at the ranges of the She-har (lions), the Corro (tigers) and the mighty Torronga (elephants), as he made his way to them. The lairs of the three great packs of beasts were situated at either side of the monkey's range, over great hot barriers, electrified fences, which kept the mighty beasts on their own lairs.

The largest animals were fed first, the little monkeys would watch in complete horror as great lumps of red, raw meat, dead animals they knew, were eaten and devoured heartlessly.

The macaques were terrified at that thought and were taught at the earliest age possible, never to stray toward the hot-wires, or venture through or beyond.

They would never return, terrible things happened there, horrible, unspeakable, in the lairs of the She-har and the Corro.

Unthinkable.

The seated humans had long since left the park, their roll-huts (cars), were now replaced with the parks low-loaders and four by fours, each filled with different containers packed with the animal's food, as they trundled through the rutted roadway.

Inside the huts, the macaques listened out for the distant humming of the motor engines, leaning over in the direction of the faint noises.

It would be soon and as usual, they could hardly contain themselves.

The Rhesus stood and watched from the highest parts of the maze of wooden limbs as he entered their hut.

He immediately looked down to the pile of assemblies and fixings that was presented for him on the floor of the hut.

One small tow-bar.

Six number plates.

Two wheel trims.

And some aerials...

He smiled softly as he bent down for a closer inspection.

Giggling quietly, he went through the mixture of grommets, fixings and trim that had been left out for him, the offering, by Maya and her pack.

She stood ten feet up from him, trying to obscure her sight from his, behind the old log which crept up to the roof; its snaking fingers of wood supported other members of the family who watched keenly on.

This was the ultimate respect from the animals to their human master, no eye-to-eye contact.

Disrespectful...

Up in the maze of branches they watched, staring silently on, the elders watchful and morose, the young ones fidgety and clinging.

He smiled to himself at the thought of the drivers of the cars; by now home and wondering what the heavens had happened to their shiny vehicles, their wash-wipe pipes, their fancy trim, their wheel covers, registration-plates?

AND A TOW-BAR!!!???

The keeper beckoned them forward, and in almost one single wave, they were upon him. They held onto his neck and shoulders, tried to climb up his legs, and basically jumped up and about in pure unbridled excitement, at all points around him. One, an imp of a female that Maya considered should have known better, actually tried to gain access into his shoulder bag, and into his little lair of special treats. The clan watched as Maya glowered at her, then the offender made her way away, munching busily as she did so.

Maya suspected that if there were to be a challenge to her supremacy, it would come from this growing, and disrespectful Chaar.

After feeding the monkeys, Har-ree examined each one for wear and tear, for cuts, lumps and bumps and signs of any infestation, as if there were ever any chance. He spoke to each of them during the inspection, tenderly, lovingly even. He had names for each one of them, but they were human pet names and of no use to the little colony of industrious simians who used their own working titles as they progressed throughout the different stages of their working lives.

They couldn't speak English anyway, understood some words but couldn't speak them, only their version of his name.

Har-ree, Harry.

They spoke a strange language.

Scottish Rhesus.

This was an eccentric mixture of different languages, dialects and accents from the original Rhesus, crazily brought about by the merging of twenty-five little monkeys from very different corners of the globe.

Four elder Macaques (three females and one male) unwanted from old run-down zoos in England.

Germany, four sad, discontented males.

Ireland, four sisters and a brother.

A male, female and two infants directly from the searing hot plains of central India.

The rest were gathered from various wildlife parks and private collections, from Aberdeen to Selkirk in the borders.

A motley, dysfunctional assortment, brought together to be part of the first Safari Park in Scotland, thirty-five long years ago.

Chapter 2

The Legend of Home

"The closest that I've been to them?"

Chee looked from his baby brother, then, darkly toward the fences.

A flash of great fear seemed to cross his eyes as he stared toward the hot-wires (electrified fences).

He then started to speak as though he were in a trance, staring over his little baby brother monkey, toward the She-har enclosure, as he mumbled slowly on...

"They can stretch their great legs through the hot-wires, they have mighty, jagged claws and they lure innocent berra (babies) toward them"

Chee then looked back to his baby brother, but through him, as if he wasn't there.

He spoke as though he was watching a terrible scene; with eyes held wide open as if in sheer terror.

He could do nothing about what he was seemingly watching.

Berra sat two feet in front of his older brother, and now he watched, beyond the open door of the hut.

Toward the hot-wire, where the terrible She-har watched and waited.

He waited and listened, wracked in growing fear.

Chee inhaled deeply as he continued to tell how the She-har hypnotize the youngsters, and then tempt them pitilessly across the fences...

He imitated the terrible beast's voice and

characteristics, and as he continued, the young one could easily envisage the scene, growing in his mind before him

The great beast smiled at him through the hot, cackling wire, with huge teeth glinting in the evening sun. It spoke to Berra, but his voice seemed so deep, it was the lowest, basest rasp, he could ever have dreamed.

"Would you like to come through?" it slowly drawled, "we have oranges and bananas in the soft beds, of our huts"

And in Berra's daydream, the great She-har slipped his mighty pad of a paw through the electrified fence, and laid it open and upturned a few feet in front of him.

Smoke singed the great beasts fur and the hot-wire cackled as tiny sparks flew from it, but the She-har felt no pain, only smiling on to the baby monkey.

The Berra now felt terror beyond belief, but could only nod dutifully toward the great beast as he continued to transfix him, with the low, hypnotic tone. He smiled again to Berra and spoke, his deep voice just under the fiercest growl the young one could imagine.

"We have warm, mother's milk, mango and pineapple little one, I know that you would love to come through, and try a little"

The little monkey was rock solid with fear, but could feel himself moving, almost floating, and closer to the great heavenly bed of a paw as it summoned him ever closer.

The softest, fluffiest of fur, the warmest of pads.....

Then, just as he was about to lay down on the great bedded fur of the paw, just as he was about to be carried away safely through the singeing cables, to the great She-har banquet of apples and oranges, the fantastic feast of pineapple, mango and Mothers milk heaven....

Glinting, gleaming claws began to appear, to extend, curve and glisten horribly in the dying light of the day, as the magnificently barbed bedposts awaited his last journey on this earth!

He screamed to the high heavens as his laughing brother shook him from the hypnotic tale he had led him into, then the young one bolted toward the sanctity and security of his mother, who had turned from a conversation with an older female, just too late to see him leap onto her and almost send her crashing to the floor, as he held on around her face and neck for dear life.

"MOTHER THE SHE-HAR, MOTHER SAVE ME!"

There was some light amusement around the hut, some adults smirked at the good natured leg-pulling and some of the older Chee monkey's laughed at the old joke played on another innocent Berra, they smiled as they remembered it, not so long ago it was them!

Berra was coaxed down from his mother after a while, but wouldn't leave her side for the next few hours or so into the early evening as the huts inhabitants grew tired and listless. Maya's Chee son had started to play again with his baby brother, tried to coax him playfully around, and back to the family fold.

There would be no need to worry about this little Berra straying close to the hot-wires, not now.

And that was the whole idea of the terrible story told to him, a great warning of where never to go...

Anywhere near the hot-wires, and the lairs of the terrible She-har and Corro.

"Why don't you tell him your story Mother, the story about home?!"

Maya looked across to Chee, she still hadn't quite forgiven him for terrorizing the small one, but she reconciled herself with the thought that Chee had only told the Berra what he had been told at the same age.

And if it kept him from wandering?

She sat upright and pulled herself from the queer mood she was in.

"About home?"

She knew what he meant, but thought she would turn the tables on her son, get him to beg her for a while.

"Yes Mother, the story you tell about home" he looked to the clan, who were mostly resting and preening, then quickly back to his mother. He spoke quietly; to make sure no one heard his request.

"You know the one I mean Mother" he whispered lowly so only she would hear what he said.

"The story of home!"

She sat with a half-smile on her face, mimicking ignorance.

"Please Mother"

"Tell me too"

She looked down to her young Berra as he suckled

"As long as it's not going to scare me"; he looked accusingly over to his older brother as he continued. His mother cupped him in as she contented him.

"No, Berra, this is a wonderful tale, told to me by my mother, and told to her by hers, many long sleeps and seasons since"

Chee watched as his mother and brother cuddled up, he was a Chee monkey now, almost fully grown.

But a little of him wanted to be in there cuddling whenever she told this tale, his most favourite, the most wondrous story, ever.

"I was only young, as young as you are just now, and it gets harder to recall it as I told it last"

She blinked her eyes, the distant memory of her mother holding into her.

Remembering.

Maya's mind rolled back the years to a time and place her mother would tell her of.

A land, a great land, of enormous plains and great forests, where the sun shines gloriously, from dawn till dusk.

Little monkeys were never cold, unhappy or hungry, a land called home.

Then other young simians listened in, almost hypnotized by the idea of the fabled land, the legend of the far off place "Of oranges and banana's, of great trees which hung over pools of cool, sweet water"

They listened intently on.

"When we were home", she imagined the generations of Rhesus, her distant forebears, living wild off the land, "We would feed ourselves with food which grew in the trees and in the long, lush grass"

She lifted her eyes to see her Chee son; by now in the glory of home, hanging onto every word she uttered, now dreaming the dream of dreams.

"Banana's hang in great bunches, just waiting for you to pick them and oranges that drip with sweet tasting juice, burst open with flavour in your mouth"

The young ones joined Chee in his fantastic dream, food was mostly hard and dried by the time it would make its way to the clans, only sometimes, fresh fruit would be available.

It was much sought after and sometimes fought over; young macaques very rarely ate fresh fruit.

They listened on.

"Your bed is made up", again she looked heavenward, motioning with her outstretched arms, "In the tallest trees, and laid with the softest leaves, so soft and sweet" she looked intently into every others eyes "you can even eat them, it's such a wondrous land"

Some adults listened on by this time, but some believed what she was saying couldn't be true, even though she was their leader.

This place was home, here with the hot-wires and the She-har, with Harr-ee (their human keeper) and the roll-houses.

Some of the elder females believed it only to be a tale, only told by mothers, eager to quieten their sleepy berra.

"It's a place where you journey over a great sea"...She looked down to the young one, "You don't know what a sea is, do you?"

The baby shook his head hopelessly, pulling his lips away from the teat to speak one milky word.

"No"...

She smiled from him and looked to the heavens.

"Could you imagine if the rain fell from the skies, and never stopped falling?"

He furrowed his brow in suspicion as he continued to feed.

"If it rained for" she stretched out ten fingers, both hands, then opened and closed her fists, imagining many times.

"All these sleeps?!"

He nodded slowly, his mind trying to imagine the

downpour.

"Could you imagine the ground filled with rainwater, with the water formed into puddles that were taller and deeper than the huts?!"

The little boy monkey shook his head in bewilderment, as he tried to envisage the deluge.

"Tell him about the Sea Dance Mother... show him"

She smiled over to Chee, who watched and listened as closely as his younger brother.

"Well", she said quite modestly, "I'm not really too sure of the Sea Dance, it was my Mothers Mother who showed me, I'm not too sure how I remember it now"

"Show him anyway"

"Yes, show me!"

The little one had stopped feeding; Maya laid him beside his brother then stood up to show them.

The Sea Dance.

She nodded to them, and then her face became set in concentration, almost a trance, as she tried to remember the Sea Dance the way her Mothers Mother had shown her.

Now the rest of the clan watched intently, as she stood in full view at the front of the children.

She outstretched her arms fully at her side, and then slowly started to limber up.

Her arms started to waiver, motioning sideways, then both limbs somehow started to oscillate, all the time, she held her chin upward. Then as she started to stand on her tip-toes, her neck and chin became fully outstretched. Her trunk and torso joined in with the movements and her body was then formed into a mass of wavering contortions. This seemed to have some kind of hypnotic effect, so much so, Chee had stood up by this time and his form copied every movement made by his mother, every fantastic oscillation, was imitated perfectly.

Then the baby joined in, standing beside his Mother and older brother.

His arms were outstretched and wavering, but his timing was quite perfect, when they motioned to the right, so did he, when they sidled forward, he magically complied.

His movements seemed instinctive, intuitive; his form matched his Mothers and Brothers exactly.

Then uncannily, the whole hut seethed and moved, as one by one, the rest of the clan's members joined in and the whole family of monkeys followed with the leader's hypnotic movements and swayed as one, to the magical Sea Dance.

The entire clan of monkeys, from the tiniest Berra, to the oldest Koth and Chaar, motioned perfectly as one, as Maya's trunk motioned forward, so would theirs, when her neck and chin flipped and swayed, so would the families.

Maya had never swam, nor had any of the family.

There was no water...

But now each member of the clan was swimming, on dry land, each one, dancing the Sea Dance.

Just as they would as if they were actually in a great sea, or lake.

And swimming upon it.

Common, instinctive, memory.

Chapter 3

The Great Escape

Chee hadn't been his usual self for the two or three days since his mother had spoken to him, to them, of her home recollections. This happened to him invariably whenever she spoke of the great place, it appeared to hang over him, at times he seemed lost in thought, as if planning, as if...

This was much to his mother's annoyance, she noticed his performance dipping, everyone had to pull their weight and work together in the clan, but now, again, he seemed as though haunted with far away thoughts and notions...

She sincerely hoped he would get over it; he was almost fully-grown and should be out of this Berra story-telling time.

This was the next working day, and he seemed distant to every other macaque.

Quietly, he found himself beside a large roll-hut and waited till the vehicle had started to slowly move off. Once out of the driver's sight, he immediately threw himself underneath, and found a shelf where he was sure he could hide during the journey.

Two Koth macaques watched on open-mouthed as the machine began to pick up a little speed, they shouted firstly to Chee, and then they bawled to Maya and the other clan members as they tried to gallop along with it.

They knew that he hadn't emerged from underneath; a check was always carried out after each task.

Eight macaques chased the vehicle toward the gates, trying frantically to catch up and release the trapped Chee monkey, but they could only watch and howl in vain as it picked up speed and raced from the enclosure, with their cousin trapped underneath!

The monkeys screamed into the morning air as they slowly lost sight of the vehicle, almost sick with distress, then they could only stare at the little spot of car in the distance.

Gathering together and almost crying with worry...

But Chee wasn't trapped.

He was lodged quite nicely, as he watched the rutted roadway pass below him.

This was what he had been planning for all his life, it seemed to him now.

He heard the desperate calls of his family, but decided it was quite funny.

It would be worth it, it could be worth anything.

To be going home.

But his easy smile ceased as the vehicle began to pick up a little speed; he sat quite transfixed as the view below him turned from the familiarity of the grassy, rutted track, where he had spent his entire life, to the tar-macked highway below him.

He stared in horror at the drive shaft as it spun and rumbled noisily beside him. Shortly after that he was clinging on for dear life, his eyes clamped tightly shut as he clutched into his little hiding place.

He had no idea where he was going to end as he zoomed away from the park.

At 76 miles, an incredible hour.

He closed his eyes as the road below him turned into a shimmering blur, he held on, now terrified beyond belief as the car took to the dual carriageway and continued on its unknown journey. It travelled on the roadway for forty long minutes, in all the time the roll-hut sped along he could only glance down, then look away in uncertainty from the flashes of black, white and yellow, the green and red dots of the cats eyes as the vehicle sped over them.

He now began to grow thoughts of his Mother and Brother, with his family of primates, as he clung to the underside of the car. He had no idea of speed and no notion of what was going on below him, so much so, at one point he tried to touch the ground flashing below and screamed in pain as the roadways surface burned into the tip of his finger when he leaned down to touch and feel it.

He sat with his finger inserted into his mouth for the rest of the journey, sucking its painful tip and ruing the moment he had made the decision to leave half an hour earlier that morning.

He froze momentarily as the car slowed and began to enter heavy traffic. He took a second to lean down and peer outside to the side of the car and could only see wheels around him. His nostrils twitched as he started to smell the emissions from the many exhausts of roll-houses which now surrounded him, he grimaced as he returned to his position at the vehicles underside.

Now he could almost taste the noxious fumes as the car started to move away from the traffic lights and travelled slowly through the town centre. The car stopped and started, went faster then slower, he clung on as tightly as he could as he watched the roadway stop, then go into reverse as the car backed into its driveway and trundled along a shale path.

Then stop...

He sat frozen in his adopted position and heard voices,

and then footsteps land on the shale.

They walked around the roll-hut.

He winced as doors were slammed and the vehicle shook for a short, last time

Footsteps...

Then, in a while, silence.

Silence.....

Breathing softly, he listened intently for any sound.

But all he could hear were the creaks and groans of the dying engine as it decompressed in the high afternoon sun.

Almost an hour after his journey had begun it had ended, and his limbs ached as he still held on underneath the car, now upside down almost, and staring around himself. He looked worriedly to the ground, the last time he had reached to touch, it had burned him.

Now there was virtual silence around him, broken only by an occasional passing car or distant laughing of children, again he bent down and looked around the car.

He held on for his dear life, making sure he wouldn't touch the scorching earth.

To his absolute amazement he saw a bird land on the shale, and looked on as it trotted busily around the car.

Holding on in the oddest of positions under the car, he down looked to the earth, it didn't look hot, but it could be deceiving.

He slowly edged his hand toward the ground and held it inches from the driveway.

No heat came from it.

He stretched a few inches further, then as quick as it takes to strike a match, he drew his forefinger along the shale and scrambled back to his retreating position.

Immediately he had his finger inside his mouth,

sucking feverishly where he imagined it would burn him.

But it didn't!

It took him fifteen seconds to summon the courage, but in the few short moments after he had touched it, he knew he had to go.

The little sparrow flew in complete surprise as the monkey bolted after falling from his hideaway and hitting the earth. He ran and jumped along the short pathway, running on his knuckles and heels, trying to protect his tender flesh from what he imagined to be the burning, scorching earth.

Then he was hiding in a little bush, which sat as a feature in an island of grass in the centre of the driveway.

Checking his fingers and toes for burns.

He gave a short, nervous, monkey smile when he saw there were none, for the first time since his escape from the park, his lips cleared his teeth confidently, but it was fleeting.

This wasn't his home; he still had to find it.

He continued to hide himself in the bush, chewing thoughtfully on his thumbnail as he tried to work out what would happen next.

She peered over her specs, looking over the page in the newspaper. Something had caught her attention in the front garden; she noticed it just in the corner of her eye.

There it was, sitting in the flowering bush and trying to hide in their front garden. She raised her voice as he climbed the stairs.

"Cats in the garden George!"

He turned in mid-step halfway up the stairs and began to return downstairs without missing a step.

A fly smile crossed her lips when she heard him

running the tap, letting the water run colder and colder. She spoke to him as he passed her line of vision in the hall.

"It's in the hydrangea bush at the front", her brows furrowed; looking over her reading specs, back in its direction.

"It's a big brown bugger!".....

Chee didn't hear the door opening.

And never noticed the slow, low crunching steps on the shale.

He turned too late to see the blanket of water about to engulf him.

The monkey screamed in shock when it hit him, then bolted away to the mixture of trees and bushes toward the rear of the large houses garden.

Now he didn't think of the burning shock of the hot earth, he was drenched in ice-cold water and quite desperate to escape from the man that stood stock-still, his hand still holding the empty jug in the position as he had thrown the water.

The man's jaws were held wide-open in shock as he watched the unknown beast disappear into the thicket of bushes and tree's. He was then completely struck dumb with the sight of its leap from the ground, and in one single bound, it was sitting on top of the old stone-built wall, six-foot high!

It turned and stared coldly back to the man for ten seconds or so, and then jumped off and ran to the common ground at the rear.

George couldn't believe what he was seeing, as it looked back and leered at him.

A MONKEY!

A BROWN MONKEY!!!...

He raced back indoors, ready to bring his wife out to witness the unbelievable...

Unfortunately, she didn't quite take it in.

She smiled hollowly over the newspaper to him, raising only one eyebrow, almost as if he was trying to tell a joke that wasn't quite funny.

"You don't get monkeys in Bearsden George.....

"Jill it was, it is!" he still stood beside the door, pointing and staring incredulously between her and the back door area.

"I saw it with my own two eyes!"

He still had the dripping jug gripped in his hand; but she shook her head nonsensically and turned back to the paper.

"It would've been a squirrel, or one of their fat-cats next door or something else, but not a monkey"...

He just stood, glaring, glowering....

Bearsden is one of the wealthier, more affluent suburbs, populated by bankers and brokers, pilots, dentists and doctors.

And Teachers and Policewomen.

They take their short-haired pointers and manicured spaniels for long, leafy walks in the parkland behind George and Jill's semi-detached villa, and explore the country walks through the common land. Their garden was an easy freeway for much of the neighbourhoods cats, and pretty much to next doors disgust, who had three cats, he attempted to soak any whenever they settled for a hunt, or a quick sniff and lick, through his garden.

He continually bombarded any intruding cats with

water, even though it had caused a broken friendship with next door.

He didn't care who noticed, they shouldn't be in his garden.

But that wasn't a cat, or a fox...it was no kind of dog.

And it wasn't a squirrel.

Or something......

George Dunbar had no idea that his neighbours had spent the afternoon at the Safari Park in Stirling, and he could never have had an inkling that a young macaque monkey could have performed such an audaciously daring act independently, and with no forward thinking or planning, other than the deep longing for the place his mother had told him of many times, the Berra tale of home.

He had acted on a whim.

Nor had he any way of discovering this amazing fact, his long running feud over next doors cats precluded any nice little over the garden fence chats about the weather and family days out. They basically ignored each other's existence to the point where they acted as total strangers, always cold and aloof when passing in their cars or the pavement.

Hence the six-foot dividing fence, newly erected by George, in a hopeless attempt to dissuade the cats from entering his property, from continually swanning through his flowered displays, and then regally marking his areas with their clinging scent.

He absolutely despised and detested them.

Consequently, if the two warring parties could communicate normally, Brian would have told George of the visit to the Safari Park, and two and two, might, have made four.

But...

Now George stood at the back wall, tiptoeing and peering hopelessly over into the copse of mixed trees and thick looking bushes all around them.

He knew he had seen it, but now, at this point?

He just couldn't prove it.

Two hours into his unexpected visit to Bearsden, Chee watched all that moved around him from his vantage point, high in a thick conifer in the copse of trees looking into the rear gardens of Luckiesfauld, the crescent of private houses where he had landed.

He watched some schoolchildren pass below him, men and women walked their dogs and at one point he pulled himself in as a dog relieved itself against the trunk of the tree he hid in.

The dog's nostrils flared, as he caught the strange scent of whatever was sitting twenty feet above him, no scent had smelled like this one before.

The dog looked up to eye the stranger that he could now see hiding in the branches above, then two front paws were on the trunk as he stretched upward for a stronger whiff of it.

He yelped annoyingly as he ran to catch up with his master who shouted for him in the distance, yes, he would remember that smell...

Eight p.m. found the young monkey cold, thirsty and hungry. He could see into the back gardens and watched through the windows as some of the families ate supper in his view.

He salivated as he watched them, unconsciously lifting

his hand to his mouth, opening his lips and chewing the imaginary food along with them.

Occasionally he would catch sight of the man who hauntingly searched over the wall.

The cold-water man.

He watched as the man ran from his door and tried to soak other small animals, but they seemed too quick and wise for him, and from this point forward, so was the monkey.

He wouldn't think about coming off the tree till light had left him, but hunger forced him down a little sooner than he would have liked, at dusk. After creeping slowly from the tree, he bolted for cover in the gathering darkness and made his way to a growth of bushes, which sat just beside the wall he had climbed over earlier that day. He crept along the back of the wall, hidden by the shrubbery that grew all along it and slowly made his way along, searching for morsels along the way. After a fruitless hundred-yard foray, he decided to scale the fence and explore the back garden areas; he would be careful and watch keenly for cold-water men. He wandered slowly in the direction of a smell, a concoction of strange aromas, and his first of many meetings with the common or garden bin.

Eight fifteen found the young monkey back up the same tree he had ventured down minutes earlier, desperately clinging onto the same branch.

He trembled, as he remembered stepping on a soft, red ball.

It squeaked as he unknowingly stood upon it.

Then a sleeping dog lifted its head and spied the monkey intruder!

Both monkey and dog recognised one another from each end of the tree in the copse, only hours earlier.

He had never heard a sound like the dogs insane bark as it chased him to the wall, at most only feet away from catching him and at least only inches from ending his short journey, the little monkey was sure he could feel the hot breath and saliva from the beast in the chilled air of the evening, as time and again it snapped at his feet and legs, and almost caught him!

He wiped his back, as if to cleanse the pursuing dog's saliva from him in his fur, and his thoughts.

Sometimes dogs were brought into the park in cars, sneaked in, and the monkeys generally considered the antics of the trapped animals foolish and empty-headed, whenever they leapt upon the roll-huts they were amused at how dogs reacted to them.

The dog may be foolish, he considered, but tonight it made the monkey look unwise and very easily, could have ended his short life.

Chapter 4

Long-Ears.

The dawn chorus awakened him, along with a gnawing hunger which had torn at his stomach for most of the long night. It had been almost a full day since his last meal, and he could feel it. He shivered awake, this was the loneliest and hungriest he had ever been. He licked dew from the moist leaves that surrounded him as he looked warily down to the back gardens.

No dogs.

The walkway to the common ground was deserted as he crept quietly down to forage for some food, now he would eat anything. He moved consciously in the opposite direction of the mad-dog and nodded to himself as he passed the area of the cold-water man; he was waiting for him to pop his head over the fence as he crawled past. The monkey had no inkling that the cold-water man was fast asleep at six fifteen a.m., Chee scurried past the larch lap, just in case. He climbed the stone wall two gardens down, at number thirty-four and looked to see what lay over, sucking his tender finger as he viewed it.

A well-filled greenhouse, a hut and a much smaller wooden hut, only as big as him, lay beside it. The simian jumped down and approached slowly, then stopped dead in his tracks when he noticed a movement inside the small hut.

Small animal...

Long ears........

Treading softly, now he was acutely aware that he was constantly in threat from various humans and animals He crept toward the little hut that sat beside the greenhouse, all the time checking around himself that he was not being watched or hunted. As he moved toward it, Chee noticed the occupant of the small hut slip back into a darkened recess, and out of his sight. When he got closer he could see the hut had a wire grill at its front.

Immediately Chee was aware that the wires would be hot, like the perimeters back at the   park

The macaque spoke to the little animal as he gingerly tapped the wires.

"Longears!"

He breathed a sigh of relief when he felt no burning sensation, then tried to peer into the darkness where the small animal lay, all the while checking around him, and thankful all was quiet and secure.

"Longears, I'm a Chee monkey.... I'm here to help you."

Still silence.

"Are you trapped?"

He still looked around himself; he was now developing awareness, a thing never required in the sanctity and security back at the park.

Chee jumped as a dull thump came from inside the recess.

"Was that you Longears?"

No reply, he looked and noticed a snib holding the door firmly shut and still looking around the back garden, he pulled it off, and opened the grilled door.

This was no difficulty really for a Chee monkey, he and his family members had been instrumental in releasing all sorts of fixtures and fittings from many types of vehicles that had entered the park, Chee had even been part of the celebrated team of simians that had found and released a spare wheel from underneath a large car.

The little monkeys were so shocked by the enormity of what they had achieved, they actually mobbed around the wheel and carried it back to the hut, they had no notion of rolling it whatsoever.

They had no idea it could be rolled; such was their confused state at the time!

Car aerials, door trim, number plates, wheel trims.

Problem solving?

No problem!

He pulled on the door and held it open, the small animal stayed out of his sight in the recess, then the sight of raw vegetables shocked him, lying around on the straw in the interior of the hut.

Immediately he grabbed a lump of turnip and started crunching on it, his first food for nearly a whole day. Then he noticed some dried food sitting in a little bowl. He pulled that out and started to stuff his face with it.

Food fell from his lips as he continued to dialogue the still hidden animal, but still watchful of his surroundings, he whispered into the darkness.

"I've opened your door Longears".

Still it was quiet.

"You can go home now!"

Then he noticed another catch, securing the solid wooden door.

He lifted it, and then pulled open the other door.

The simian held his tender finger in his mouth as he viewed, for the first time, the inhabitant of the little hut.

A small Netherlands dwarf rabbit.

"There you are"...

The rabbit munched nonchalantly on a sprig of straw.

Chee was almost dumbstruck, the little animal didn't attempt to move or escape his confinement! He finished the last morsel of veg. as he tried to reason with it.

"You're free!"

It sat silently, nibbling.

"Go home!!!"

Eileen Harker had let herself quietly out of her back door and walked to the washing line. She started to pin up the small amount of damp clothes, not taking too much notice in the six thirty silence. Although it was very early to be awakened, it was a beautiful morning and sometimes, especially on mornings as this, she considered it to be the nicest part of the day, daybreak.

And now the baby was back asleep so she could appreciate this time of the growing morning.

She smiled at the birdsong, and the day broke beautifully as she hung up young Jamie's baby clothes.

Then she froze as she noticed something stir.

It moved slowly, nestling into her soft carpet slippers.

"Bobby!"

She looked unbelievingly down to her daughter's rabbit, and then spied his hutch doors.

Open.

She picked him up and stroked him, gently whispering.

"How did you get out, little man?"

She inspected the hutch doors as she placed him back inside; and was quite disturbed to see that both doors had been freed, from the outside.

No food left inside his hutch...not a morsel!

He watched her as she placed Longears back inside the

cage, he couldn't believe it had the chance to escape and go home...but he chose to remain. His features were a picture of intense concentration, as he watched the lady and the long eared one.

Eileen had no idea she was being spied upon as she looked around, just as the little beast had done in the gathering morning, she figured whoever...or whatever, had let wee Bobby out, was probably long gone by now.

Stepping back into the kitchen, she gave the back garden a wary look.

It was a very, very, strange situation.

Chapter 5

Old Hector.

"Hector, congratulations! It's an absolute cracker".

The old man nodded in proud agreement." Thanks son," he agreed," It is good to see it all finished".

Both men stood a few feet from it, Peter cupping his chin so it wouldn't drop off, and old Hector, arms folded in relaxed pose.

"These things were the hardest to find out of the whole re-assembly", Hector looked over the rims of his specs and tapped a rear view mirror, he shook his head as he continued" I had to trawl a scrap yard in Cardiff to get a hold of these".

The young man nodded appreciably.

"Still Hector, if you're going to do it right, it's always worth it ", he looked back to the old man and gave him an encouraging pat on his shoulders, "And you always do!"

Both men stood nodding their heads for a second or two more.

"To think that this was the same piece of scrap that you picked up in that farm in Eaglesham".

"I know".

"Who'd have thought that two years later, it would have been turned into, this!"

"I know".

It sat in front of them, a 1958 Triumph Bantam 600 cc motorcycle, completely rebuilt and reconditioned.

The British racing green paintwork was fresh and sheened, the chromium steeled wheels and exhaust gleamed in the garage strip light.

The speedometer stated zero!

He watched the two men as they spoke. They had absolutely no idea that they were being spied upon by a year old Rhesus monkey, newly escaped from a Safari park forty miles away. They carried on with their conversation.

Chee was hidden from their sight, resting high inside a half empty box, which sat above old Hectors overall locker. From his vantage point, high in the corner of the concrete garage, he eyed all that was around him. The garage was a treasure trove of industrious paraphernalia and gadgets, tools and various spare parts, which the old guy had collected, in a very busy lifetime of seventy-five years.

He was always doing odd jobs; his garage and hut were littered with little favors that he would take on for friends and family.

Shadow boards filled with tooling were attached to the walls. Saws of every description hung on mounts.

Screwdrivers, socket sets, rows of spanners, wrenches and crimping pliers. The old man's garage was an industrious guddle of tooling, but it was an organized guddle.

A place for everything and everything in its place, so much so, whenever Hector was asked to lend someone a tool, he could immediately lay his hands on it, and probably even blindfolded.

R.A.F. Training.

Twenty five years of it.

The little simians breathing was slow and shallow, his metabolic rate halved, as he lay above them and viewed all that went around him.

Tool heaven, he could imagine that this was what Harree would do with the gadgets offered by the clan, back at the safari park. Chee gulped slowly in awe, and then watched as the old man motioned the younger to sit on the machine. Young Peter was delighted when Hector invited him to start the engine, he turned the key, then kick-started it.

The little beast was almost thrown from his hideout; such was the shock he received as the Bantam was sparked into life!

The 600 cc engine block cascaded the garage walls floor and ceiling with an ear-bursting roar, and then filled the air with the thick nauseous smoke as old Hector twisted the accelerator in the handgrip, droning loudly in the concrete confines.

Luckily both men had their backs to the monkey and were unaware of him as he visibly jumped with the shock of the start-up. Then again, he started to sniff and recognized the dreadful gasses, as the engines exhaust quickly began to fill the air in the garage. The motorcycles exhaust blew directly into the area, which Chee occupied behind the two men.

Just as the Macaque was starting to contemplate escape, when he thought he could take no more of the noxious gasses, which had lifted and gathered to form a poisonous, bilious, blue cloud just at his height, the old man leaned over and turned off the engine.

He watched as they shook hands, then both of them made their way away. Chee was relieved that the door had been left open, and was duly grateful when fresh air began to waft in, he felt invigorated as the cold air began to circulate and break up the murk which had overtaken the atmosphere, he was thankful and sucked in gulpfuls of the cool fresh air.

The old man returned a few minutes later, carrying a plate with two delicious looking sandwiches and a mug of steaming, black tea. Just as he sipped at the mug, the monkey heard a strange ring in the distance, then the old man arose from his crouching position at the bikes brake column and walked off in the direction of the ringing.

He heard the man's voice in the distance and two minutes later Hector returned.

The man stretched his hand in the direction of the sandwiches, but was stunned to feel then see the plate was empty!

The black contents of his mug swilled gently, some liquid was spilled at the base of the mug...

He looked up suspiciously and his eyes tracked the interior of the stillness of the garage.

The little beast held his breath as the old man again laid his open hand and padded the empty plate.

Nothing...

He stepped to the door and checked around the back door area.

No dogs...

Or cats...

Old Hector couldn't figure it out, he definitely had not eaten them, could see no trace of any other animal, maybe bird's he considered.

He gave the interior a strange, last look as he switched off the light then locked the door, Chee saw him but the old guy could have no inkling of what lay in his garage as he entered the kitchen and started to butter some more bread.

The monkey licked at his burnt lips, and tried to

soothe them with his moist tongue.

But that burned too!

How he desired to have cold water, at that point he would have licked from a puddle.

Or let the cold-water man soak him!

He screwed his eyes and tried breathing quickly with his lips clear of his teeth; again he had been shocked by a very hot sensation.

For the first half hour he sat in the box, convinced the old man would return. Then he tentatively climbed down and started to explore the garage with only a thin shaft of moonlight to give him any guidance. His feet soon became cold on the hard stone floor and he grued at the strange smell that clung to his fingers from the wheels of the machine. The machine made a natural climbing frame and the young macaque soon found himself at rest on the soft seat quite by accident.

For the first time that day, he felt at ease, the seat quickly warmed to his body temperature, with his stomach full and satisfied, he curled into a ball on the seat and watched the full moon as clouds flitted past.

Fleetingly, Chee thought of his mother and brother, he wondered if she was watching the moon at the same time as him. He closed his eyes as tiredness started to creep upon him.

Sleep   overcame   him   just   after   midnight.

Chapter 6

Intruder in the Midst!

Old Hector stopped dead in his tracks as he walked around his back garden.

The small window in his garage was open; it flapped loosely in the light wind.

How the heck?

He thought to himself, that window always remains closed, he knew the window was too small for any access, but a child?

Hector walked to it, then pulled it open and looked inside the garage.

It looked clear enough, nothing seemed amiss and the old Triumph motorcycle still stood where he had last attended it.

Then he noticed something sitting on the far side of the bike; some stuff lay on the concrete floor, just at the side door.

A little pile of metal bits and bobs?

The old guy rushed to the back door of the house and grabbed the keys from the holder, now his very inquisitive mind was racing sixteen to the dozen, no he definitely didn't open it last!

And just what was lying at the door??

Hector inserted the key, turned it, and then slowly drew the door open.

He stood clear and waited for any movement from it, by birds or animals unknown.

It soon became clear; the garage was empty, thankfully.

The incident from last night, with the missing

sandwiches and spilled tea flashed to his mind, then he looked to the floor.

A number-plate and a wheel hubcap...

Hector gave the inside of the garage a very thorough examination, all his tools were intact and the bike, the pensioner's most treasured possession in the garage, lay exactly as he had left it.

But the window?...

He approached it and stood by it for a few moments while he thought about it.

The number-plate and hubcap, arrived through this window, somehow...

He pushed it open, then tried to push his head and shoulders through.

No way.

He pulled it closed then snibbed it again. The old man picked up the hub cover, number-plate and held them as he went to exit the door.

Then Hector noticed some hairs on the seat of the motorbike, long brown hairs, he wondered as he examined the clump.

Was it animal hair?

The pensioner locked the garage and walked off with the keys, number-plate, wheel trim and the little clump of fur/animal hair and just before he left the garage, he unfastened the small window, leaving it dangling in the wind, just as was found.

For it was just then Hector Kerr realised that he was being visited, and smiled to himself at the thought.

Chapter 7

Monkey Business

The old man had always been very handy, very good with his hands.

He had laid the concrete foundations and assembled the garage by himself, erected the carport just in front of it and built from scratch, the gazebo style hut, his own design, which lay on the far side of the back green.

Always decorated the house himself, looked after his own garden, and serviced his own car, three times a year.

No job was too big or too small for this old guy, who had nothing but time on his hands.

So when he started to buy electrical leads, contacts and a small amount of batteries, no one asked any questions, everyone was always used to this busy, pottering pensioner and his industrious ways.

He attached the contacts, one on the windowsill inside the hut, and the other on a thin board fashioned to sit a few centimetres above the sill, then to make contact the moment any weight was put upon it.

Even if it were only a few grams, it was designed to make contact.

A connecting wire was led from this point of contact to the apex of the garage roof, then on to the upstairs window; where it would light a small bulb inside Hectors bedroom, when the contacts were triggered.

And Hector did have time aplenty, even before he decided that he was going to pursue his unknown visitor. In the long dark winters evenings he would read for ages, regularly finishing a book that held his interest, from start to finish overnight.

Hector usually only slept for five or six hours, so was ready for a long wait as he had settled into his hard chair, book in hand and flask by his side, at ten twenty.

As light was beginning to fade outside, he put on a small reading lamp and started on the book.

Hector was astounded when the light flashed before the end of the first chapter!

It went on, then off.

Then on for a longer spell, then off!

Immediately he pulled his curtain open a little, and then viewed the garage, but save the flapping window, there was nothing.

Silence.

He turned the reading lamp off then pulled the curtains open a little more and stood waiting to catch sight of the brown haired intruder.

The light started to flicker, to shine momentarily, then went off.

He felt his heart thud in his breast, but not with fear or trepidation; this was unbridled excitement, he didn't remember having feelings like this, since he was a child!

He waited almost ten minutes, wiping the window every few minutes or so as the condensation from his breath and body vaporised on the glass, but suddenly the light flickered, and remained on!

Then through the misty glass, he saw movement....

He watched in absolute wonder as the window levered up, then a long hairy arm held it open!

The pensioner stretched for a tissue to wipe the glass, it was steaming up again.

Hector smiled so much at that point, he almost

laughed aloud.

Such was his sense of awe, a little tear of such unknown joy trickled down his face, he dabbed his moist cheek with the wet tissue as he watched in wonder.

And just as he did so,

He saw...

A monkey climb from the window!

Chapter 8

The Fridge Magnet.

Three days out of the park and the little monkey still lived in and around the area where he had first fell from the underside of the Range Rover. From his viewpoint high in the copse of trees, he was now quite familiar with his neighbours in Leggat Drive and Baird Walk. First of the row of large family houses was a young family with three children, all girls. Their father worked away from home for a month at a time; currently he was in his second week away. Then another younger couple, no children, both worked all day, returning later in the evening.

Next was an old couple, both retired.

Then the mad dogs house, a frisson ran across his back, he shivered momentarily when the thought of the dog crossed his mind. Then another couple with no children, this was the house that he had first arrived at in Leggat Drive when he had crept from the under-side of the Range Rover, so full of hope.

Next was the cold-water man, he swallowed bitterly at the sight of that house.

Then another family, two children, older, maybe both in high school and both boys, followed by an old lady, who had a yappy, spoiled little dog, the kind they loved back at the park.

It yapped incessantly, whenever the old lady left it alone, next was a small, young family with a little baby and the Longears, and lastly, the old man with the machine in the garage.

The monkey couldn't realize that he had landed in

quite an affluent area, but people didn't spend an awful lot of their time talking or passing the time of day, so any strange goings on were usually quite slow to be picked up, if at all.

He hadn't taken any time to explore the front of the houses, that was where he was drenched and since then, he had seen dogs, his biggest fear, walking unrestrained. He regarded himself in a safer position at the rear of the houses, in the little forest of trees and overgrown bushes.

He could safely scale a tree in seconds, and he knew that dogs couldn't.

Twelve o'clock found him baking in the sun high up on the thin poplar. This was the hottest August that had been recorded for nearly thirty five years and after almost ten days of unbroken sunshine, he was discovering that the Scottish climate can be as severe in a blazing July or August noon, as it could be in a January cold snap, of ten degrees below.

At twelve-thirty he could stand the overpowering heat no longer and started to slowly pick his way down and off the tree. The family with the three girls had been lying out, soaking in the sun's rays and being the closest ones to him, he had watched as they ate and drank copiously from the white box in the house.

Orange coloured water, fruit, apples bananas and pears.

And many other things.

All in the white box.

Birds and insects droned busily in and around the massed borders, rockery and hedging, the garden was well secluded and fenced off by thick rose hedging on one side and a continuous growth of Leylandi hedging, cropped at ten feet on the other.

The soft sound of the children's radio wafted lazily over the walls and back door greenery and Chee listened curiously as the girls, at twelve, ten and four years of age, sang along and sometimes danced, to their favourite music. He stood, nestled in a thick bush, his eyes peering over the stonewall.

The monkey looked through the open kitchen door, the mother was preparing a little lunch, some salad and cold savoury rice.

He watched hungrily as she lifted everything in and out of the fridge, the white box. Sometimes she would leave the door open while she worked away, he could only guess at the wonders which lay inside it.

Mother stepped in and out of the kitchen, laying the places and condiments, all the while; the macaque salivated in his hidden position, not fifteen feet from the table.

The middle child had started to complain about the unremitting heat, she wore hats, sunglasses, lay on the lounger, then on the grass, but the heat was still clinging, stifling.

Her mother tried coolly to reprimand her.

"It's not that, when you can't get out for the rain, when it drizzles down for days at a time!"

The daughter pulled off the hat that covered her face.

"That would be excellent", she exclaimed, opening her hands and extending her arms to accept the imaginary downpour, "If it could rain a little now, even just a little shower..."

Mother stared at her as she passed by with a tray, full of plates, then she continued with the rebuke.

"And what happens when there's three feet of snow,

sometimes its so bad you cant even go to school!"

Then the oldest piped in, "Three feet of snow??!!" She yelled, "And no school???!!!"

The three sisters laughed aloud as they shouted the word in unison.

"EXCELLANT!!!!"

Mother happily feigned disgust at her hot and happy brood, while the unusual afternoon sun continued to blaze unabated.

He watched them all as they sat around the table and chair set, sheltered only by a small parasol. The middle child had made sure she sat directly below it; the rest only enjoyed partial shading.

They slowly picked at their food, and yet again Lorna moaned about the heat. Mother pulled up her magazine and read on, only nibbling at her food as she read.

Lunchtime passed slowly that afternoon and the only one to keep active was the youngest, Tracy. After one more hour in the heat, they slowly peeled off, one by one, back into the comparative coolness of the house.

He couldn't take his eyes off the remains of the luncheon.

He spied a slice of tomato.

A sprig of spring onion.

Green lettuce

Then he could see the jug of coloured water and handfuls of cold rice on one plate.

Lorna's.

This was enough for a complete banquet, a feast for a little monkey!

In less than three seconds, he was over the wall and behind a chair, still watching where the family departed.

He looked from behind a draped towel to the food.

So close.

Now he could actually smell it, he knotted his eyebrows as a little bird landed on the table and started to peck at the scraps of rice. He readied himself to go, but the bird held itself.

Movements inside.

"I'll clear up the mess for a wee change girls, shall I?"

He stared in horror as she strode from the kitchen and marched up to the chair that hid the monkey. His features screwed in despair as she held the plates up and emptied the scraps of food into a black bin bag.

NO!

He shook his head under the table.

He had to slide quickly under the chair when she walked around it to tidy the far side, but after one minute she left the site, a pile of dishes cups and cutlery on the tray.

Chee watched her enter the kitchen, and then quite boldly, lifted his head to check out the table top.

Complete disappointment was etched on his face as he discovered it spotlessly cleaned of all traces of the monkey feast, if monkeys could ever swear, he would have then.

He could see the mother work about the kitchen, every time she entered the white box, he salivated. She brought an apple from the fridge, and then crunched into it.

The little simian could hear every bite she made on the piece of chilled fruit and duly chewed along with her.

Then she was gone out of his sight.

He moved quickly to the lounger that was closest to the kitchen door, pulling the towel from his previous hideout and draping it over himself as he ran across the open grass.

The little animal tried to use a form of camouflage!

He just made it when, again he had to freeze.

Someone entered the kitchen; he pulled himself in and then screwed his eyes to peek through the slats on the back of the chair, the little girl, the smallest one.

He watched her intently as she skipped over to the white box and pulled the door wide open.

She pulled a carton from it, and then took her plastic glass from the rack. The animal's eyes were transfixed on the contents of the fridge as the child poured herself a drink. For the first time, he could see it in detail, and it did look wondrous.

Bottles, packages, fruits, sauces and juices.

And much more!

The macaque watched on from behind the door, fascinated by what appeared before him, then after a few moments, the child was gone, trailing back to watch television.

But she had left the carton on the table top!

And the fridge door open!!

Slowly and carefully, he moved from the back door, cautiously checking that no one was still in the kitchen.

He didn't know where to start, the white box thing lay tantalisingly open, displaying it's wealth of food and drink, but the child had left the carton of delicious looking juice out, so he thought he would start there.

There was only one problem, he had never drunk from a carton, nor any kind of receptacle, the monkey's had all drunk from a communal trough, back home at the Park. He leapt onto the work surface and sniffed the carton.

It smelled wonderful.

The little simian shook the carton and it swilled over the spout, forming into a little puddle of juice at his feet.

He lapped up the puddle, and then spilled some more.

Fantastic!

All the time he was drinking, he was watching. His eyes darted from the carton to the door, and from there to the beautiful white box and its wonderful contents. He had drunk nearly a third of the carton of juice then lifted it and for the first time, attempted to drink from it.

He only succeeded in drenching himself completely, at first the cold liquid shocked his senses, then he enjoyed the cold sensation on the hot summer's day. Chee erected himself, and from the puddle of juice that he stood dripping in, he again looked over to the fridge, with the door hanging invitingly open.

Jumping down, the simian ran quickly over, now standing underneath it at the level of the lower freezer.

Chee looked up and almost worshipped the sight above him, thirst quenched, now he was about to satisfy his weltering hunger.

The simian picked his way up, then found himself resting with one foot on the closed freezer door and the other on the fridges bottom shelf. The first thing he could identify was an apple, invitingly chilled and moist. He snatched a mouthful and immediately his eyes were drawn to a sight a foot away from him, a fresh trifle made by Mother the day before, for dinner tonight. He dropped the apple after one bite and it fell beside the empty carton. One hand grabbed a banana and the other was pulled, as if by a strange magic, to the magnificent sight of the trifle! He unpeeled the banana with one hand, his teeth and lips and bit hungrily into it.

Then he poked his digit into the creamy top, sprinkled with hundreds and thousands.

He moved his finger around the cream, then pulled it out and slowly sniffed it as he chewed on the second bite of the banana.

The feel and the texture of the cream fascinated the little beast, and as he tried to sniff the white glob from his finger, a spot of it stuck on his nose.

He grued on his first tasting of the cream, then for the first time in his short monkey life, he tasted sweetness, and it was beautiful. His hand was inserted straight back into it and he continued to pleasure himself in the new sensation of sweetness. He ate handfuls of the globby mixture of custard, cream and the fruity tasting sponge; so much so, his face was soon a mass of white, red and yellow from its contents, as were both his paws. The little animal was so engrossed with the trifle and all the other temptations, he didn't hear the door being opened, and he definitely didn't see the middle child, Lorna Ann, enter the kitchen.

She was just about to pull up her four year-old baby sister for leaving the fridge door opened, when she saw the mess at the foot of it.

Then she was astounded to see a partly eaten banana getting thrown from the half-closed fridge.

Now it was apparent, something was in the fridge!

She held her breath in check and tip-toed toward the open door, still she couldn't see inside the fridge, as the door was open side on, facing away from her.

The monkey was beyond any help by this time, the trifle lay in tatters; he had also tried to eat from a margarine pack and immediately wiped it from his tongue in disgust.

Again this was thrown from the fridge!

He didn't know a thing about it, he only heard a half-scream and then turned just in time to see the fridge door slam in his face.

Chee sat in total darkness, wedged in between shelves, and frozen in position as he stretched over to investigate another smell and taste.

Now his drenched body started to feel cold as the juice that had earlier refreshed and engulfed him, now chilled him. His little body then started to shake, a mixture of the coldness that he was experiencing in the darkness of the closed fridge, and the unknown situation he had found himself drawn into.

He had no idea what would happen next!

Lorna-Ann burst into the living room and stood just inside it, straddling the open doorway. Ashen faced, eyes almost popping from her sockets, for the first time that day, she was unable to speak!!

Unfortunately, no-one seemed impressed.

"What's wrong with you now!" her Mum had almost had enough of her, by this point, "you've been a little horror all day!"

Her sisters continued watching television; Lorna-Ann had to force it out.

"Mum?"

It wasn't quite clear yet; she looked back toward the kitchen and reminded herself

"Mum!"

Now her voice was just above a whisper.

"Mum

There's

a

monkey

in

the

fridge!"

Hazel looked irritably to her sister, then quickly away from her.

"We're trying to watch this Lorna, will you just go away!"

Lorna-Ann was beside herself by this time, a monkey was in their fridge.

And no-one would believe her!!!!

She strode past her Mum and sisters, stood slap bang in front of the TV. and shouted for as loud and as long as her voice would register.

"MOTHERRR!"

"THERE'S!"

"AAAA!"

"MONKEYYY!"

"INNN!"

"THHHE!"

"BLOODYY!"

"FRIIIDGGGE!!!!!"

This had an immediate effect, and just as Mother was about to raise herself, Lorna-Ann ran in the direction of the kitchen, followed closely by her Mother and siblings.

She ran to the far side of the kitchen and stood by the back door.

Then her Mum entered the room; sisters right behind her, all very aggrieved with the very irritable Lorna-Ann.

They stopped the second they saw the mess on the floor, little Tracy was visibly shocked at the jumble of discarded containers on the floor.

"Mummy, look at that mess!"...

Mother looked from the pile of half eaten-food and packages then doggedly turned to Lorna-Ann.

"If this is your idea of a joke young lady!"

Lorna-Ann stood, still looking incredulously at the closed door of the fridge, and shaking her head hollowly as she spoke.

"Mum...Open the door!"

Her Mother leered at her, then turned to the fridge, waiting, just ready for some stupid stunt pulled by her daughter. This kind of thing had happened before with her and her older sister, but now?

Hazel seemed quite detached from any would be prank.

Mother still growled at her as she swung the door open

"This had better be good young lady, really good!"

As she swung the door open, she saw a look of total bewilderment on her daughter's faces.

Then, Mother turned slowly around to see what was causing the look of horror...

To her utter disbelief, a little beast lay wedged in between the shelves and took a full ten seconds or so to extricate himself.

Then he turned to see the gallery of bewildered humans that watched him, all four of them, absolutely speechless!

When the monkey manoeuvred himself around they could see for the first time, that it was indeed, a living, breathing beast that had made its way into their home.

Then into the fridge.

The fur around his face was covered in a sponge, cream and jam mixture, but it was only when he tried to communicate, pathetically, with the females, that the heavens broke.

He tried to say.

"I'm only a Chee monkey, I mean you no harm, and I respect your hut"

But he was so frightened and worked up; it just came out as;

"AAAAAAAAARRRRRRRGGGGGGHHHHHHH HH!!!"

To be perfectly fair, the reaction of the females of the Muir household was exactly the same and for ten seconds or so, every living and breathing thing in the kitchen screamed, for as long and as loud as they could, with the little macaque probably making as much of a racket as the females.

But luckily for him, he was first to react.

He bolted past the shrieking ladies of the house and took refuge where it made most sense to him.

Up the stairs of course, cause humans can't climb as well as monkeys.

They stood back in uncertainty as he leapt past them, none of them had ever seen a monkey up close before, never mind finding one in your fridge, so they were partly relieved to see it race away.

But up their stairs???

Up the stairs to their rooms???!!!

The children turned instantly to their Mother for guidance as they shouted together, almost as one voice.

"IT'S UPSTAIRS MUM!!!"

She nodded manically to them, and they closed ranks as Mother gathered them together at the bottom of the stairs.

And there it was, as clear as day, a little trail of jam, cream and custard left by the macaques paws as he bolted upstairs.

There on every fourth step, were two prints.

Two little smudges of red, white and yellow....

The kids pulled and squealed at their Mother, each offering pearls of advice.

"Better phone the R.S.P.C.A. Mum!" advised Hazel

"Mummy, phone Daddy!" whispered little Tracy.

And.

"Let's go up and see it Mum!"...from Lorna-Ann, who by this time, was well up for it!!

A real, live monkey in the house!!!

They were still trying to make up their minds, still trying to figure out what best to do first.

When they heard the first crash!

The three older ones stared in horror to each other, then little Tracy gave out a short, sharp scream!

Lorna-Ann had her hands covering her face.

"That's my c.d. rack!"

Another clatter, then little Tracy looked in a flash to her Mummy.

"That's my goldfish bowl Mummy, He's spilled out wee Harry!!!"

The whole lot of them raced up stairs, as soon as she uttered the words, the ladies frantically trying to save wee Harry the goldfish, they arrived at the top of the landing as one almost, with little Tracy coming up last, holding onto her Mothers shirt-tail.

They grouped together at the top landing and shuffled forward to the place where the trail of paw-prints led.

Lorna-Ann and Tracy's room!!

First on the right....

There were no noises; the top landing was completely silent, save the heavy breathing and hushed whispers of the Muir ladies as they approached the room.

Mother was first to poke her head into view, then Hazel just below hers.

Then Lorna-Ann, and just below hers?

Little Tracy....

Apart from a mass of paw-prints, there were no outward signs of the monkey; the room seemed eerily quiet, and still.

Then the little goldfish flipped on the floor, splashing on the remains of the water soaked up by the carpet. Lorna-Ann was first to enter, actually running into the room, with seemingly no regard to herself, she was determined to save wee Harry.

She picked him up in cupped hands and plopped him into the shallow pool that remained in the bowl, all the time, she and her Mother and sisters watched warily around the room.

Waiting for it to appear.

Lorna-Ann lifted the bowl and placed it on the dresser with her Mother and sisters standing back to back around her.

All.

Watching.

All anyone could hear was the light splashing coming from the goldfish bowl as Harry tried to swim in the shallow pool.

Hazel saw it first, mouth agape, staring in urgency toward her bed, and pulling at her Mothers shirt.

She had to be sharp to notice him, but Hazel always

was.

"Mother"...she whispered, staring and pointing toward it.

"Under The Quilt!".....

They turned as one to look.

Hazel had a lime coloured, floral quilt, with some soft toys scattered upon it.

But there was a definite lump at the top just beside the pillow.

"LOOK MUM!!" urged Hazel, tugging further and pointing in urgency toward the top of the bed.

When you looked closely, very closely, you could make out the quilt slowly raising, and then lowering.

The Muir girls realised the monkey was lying under the quilt, and breathing shallowly. They again looked directly toward their Mother, each one silently pointing toward the lump on the bed, and waiting for advice...

Mother gave her measured response in whispered, even tones.

"Lorna-Ann, you get the top right hand of the quilt, Hazel, you get the left hand"

Both moved slowly into position.

"Tracy, can you hold this little bit darling?"

She handed the bottom left corner of the duvet to the youngest daughter.

"Now just hold it down sweetheart"...

She continued as she slipped quietly to the last corner.

"When I nod my head, we'll just pull it all together, then we can tie it up"

She nodded in agreement to each of her daughters.

They returned the nod, then each inhaled heavily, awaiting the instruction from Mother...

Now, if Mother thought this was going to be quick, and easy manoeuvre, that they would be able to effortlessly tie up the monkey in the quilt??

She inhaled one last time, and then nodded.

Once again, the room broke into bedlam, each one of the females pulled their corner down and over to the opposite side, but the monkey quickly broke free and found himself standing on top of the bed with the four would be monkey-hunters on each side of him.

Again he and they screamed at the very sight of each other for the few seconds they found themselves together, another round of mutual screaming!!

And then he was gone.

The ladies again followed the simian as he ran in the direction of the biggest and brightest room upstairs.

Mum and Dads room!

All the time that this was happening, the Muir's had no inkling that the front door had just been tapped and opened from the outside, with Mrs. Muir's sister arriving; as usual she just let herself in.

The visitor waited and listened.

"HI JANE, IT'S ONLY ME!"

She smiled to herself when she heard the tumult from upstairs, she thought the whole family were running down to meet her, and was quite pleased at that notion!

But she couldn't have been more wrong.....

Listening a little closer, the visitor heard the family run from across the top landing it seemed...

Shouting...and...bawling...as they ran??

From room to room???

Then she heard a noise over the others.

Squealing, a strange howling from above??

Susan heard them run as one, from the back bedrooms to the front, then to the top of the stairs.

A thunderous clatter as the entire houses occupancy ran down to meet her.

"DON'T OPEN THE DOOR SUSAN!!"

"KEEP THE DOOR SHUT AUNTIE SUSAN!!!"

And just as the shocked Auntie Susan was about to do so, just as she had her hand on the door, to blindly close it.....

A monkey rounded the corner at the bottom of the stairs!

Auntie Susan gasped at the very sight of it!!

He spun on his heels, and turned to face her!!!

A BROWN RHESUS MONKEY!!

FACE AND HANDS COVERED IN A SLIMY MIXTURE OF CUSTARD, CREAM AND JAM!

He spied the open front door as his exit, and raced by her.

As he sped past, the completely bewildered Auntie Susan nearly collapsed at the sight before her!

Then Lorna-Ann turned at the bottom of the stairs, and chased after it.

"It's a monkey, Auntie Susan!!!"

Next, it was Aunty Susan's sister, the girl's Mother, who raced by the stricken Auntie and held a net curtain upward, in a valiant attempt to snare the little animal. She was followed closely after by Hazel.

Both raced doggedly past, and ran to follow Lorna-Ann, yelling as they followed up!

Then little Tracy ran by, shouting and pointing toward the rapidly disappearing beast.

"It's a monkey Auntie Susan; we found it in our

fridge!!!"

And just then, Auntie Susan did, collapse...

Chapter 9

A First Brush.

"Hello Mister Paterson, I think these things may belong to you"

He smiled to the younger man as he held out the wheel trim and number plate. Alex Paterson looked slightly bemused, accepting them without speaking at first.

He had noticed the wheel trim missing, but the number plate?

His voice lowered in suspicion.

"Yes...they are off... my car"...

Old Hector smiled then turned to walk off, but Alex had a question.

"How did you...where did you find them, Mister Kerr?"

Hector turned at the bottom of the path, explaining while locking the gate.

"I think there's a wee monkey around here that likes to collect these things"

He walked off smiling broadly, leaving the younger man no wiser than when he rapped his door in the first place.

And probably more confused...

George Dunbar stood at the open window, hiding just behind the curtains, and quite dumbstruck!

His eyes and mouth, wide-open in disbelief.

Or was it re-belief?

He heard the old man say it, a wee monkey that stole

hubcaps and number plates!

Immediately his mind raced back to the scene some days ago when he thought he had chased a cat from his front garden, but it was a monkey, he watched it as it climbed the fence, then it stared back to him for some moments.

Both, watching each other!!

HE COULD STILL PICTURE IT!

Was it the monkey? Was this valediction?

Sergeant Paddy MacAskill was having a very bad day. It began the previous evening, when his ten year-old son started coughing and through the course of the night it became so course and rough, it was more like a dogs bark.

OW! OW! OW! OW!

They gave him medicine, a sleeping draught mostly, at ten, but he returned at eleven, "Can't sleep Mum...OW! OW! OW!"

Then he started to sound more like a sea-lion, Paddy and his wife saw every hour on the clock that night, and when he left to go to work at seven, he was greeted by the sadly deflating sight of a flat-tyre on his car.

OW! OW! OW!

Now this stupid woman was telling him that she had a monkey that had just run around her house, wrecking the kitchen and bedrooms!?

He held out the phone, staring ridiculously at it, then he rubbed his bristled chin as he attempted to dialogue with her.

"This...Monkey...Mrs Muir..." He shook his head as he spoke, with his pen raised indecisively over the blank sheet, "Eh, what colour was it?"

He could hear a mass of children's voices on the other

side of the phone, then it occurred to him; they were all listening on the other end!

"It was red"

Then children's voices became raised and excited.

"Red? Mrs..."

"Reddish ...brown!"

He thought the whole thing was becoming quite ridiculous and felt like saying so.

It was actually a waste of Police time.

"This little reddish, brown monkey Mrs...."

"Muir"

"Mrs. Muir, don't you think it was maybe more like a squirrel or something?"

"No Constable, it was definitely a monkey!"

Constable??? he grued his face.

The pen still twirled above the blank report sheet with only the name, Muir, and the word monkey, followed by a serious of question marks added to it.

"So, definitely a monkey Mrs. Muir", now he felt like becoming a little silly, as desk Sergeants sometimes do.

"But it wasn't large?"

"No Constable!"

Const?...

"So it wasn't a chimpanzee"

"No Constable"

"Or a baboon!"

Paddy thought he heard what sounded like a wrestling, scuffling noise on the other end. Then a new, young voice announced itself.

"Hello Constable"

"Sergeant!"

"My name is Lorna-Ann Muir and this animal wasn't a

chimpanzee, a baboon or even a gorilla, as you're probably going to ask next, but a brown Rhesus Macaque monkey, standing about forty centimetres high!"

He remained quiet, quite in shock, as she continued.

"It has caused havoc in my bedroom and all the other rooms in our house, so whether you believe my Mother and me or not, my Father is due back from the oil-rigs on Wednesday and if something's not done about this, I'll bring him around to the station to see you himself, so do you think you could do something about it?

He was aghast!

She had caught him right out, his tongue felt the size of an inflatable life-raft!

The girl, Lorna-Ann continued as the desk Sergeant tried to lift his jaw from the floor.

"Now, PLEASE!"

Sergeant MacAskill was then forced reluctantly, to take note of the whole unlikely scenario, staring from the report sheet, to the high heavens, in equal measures.

And on Thursday 12th August, at 15 45, the first report of a loose, brown macaque was filed at Bearsden Police Station.

Chee's first brush with the law.

Chapter 10

The Ballaholic.

He sat resting in the shade of an overgrown rhododendron, over the walls at the rear of the houses. The thought of the family of females trying to catch him was quite confusing to him, they didn't seem aggressive, but they did try to catch him. What would have happened after that, maybe they wanted to eat him, he didn't know....

It was over now anyway and as he reflected on the goings on of the afternoon, he still had some creamy mixture caked around his face and forearms, so he just sat there, just happy to lick it off in the coolness of the shade.

This was the nicest taste in the world!

What he didn't know, was that when he had raced from the Muir's, Mrs. Davidson was washing dishes at her sink and looked up just as he had raced over the dividing fences between the two gardens.

She stared on in disbelief at the sight which took only a few seconds to pass her back door area and drying green.

She spent a moment deep in incredulous thought.

Was it?...

No...

She ended up thinking it must have been the ugliest cat she had ever seen in her life.

So for now, was all quiet and calm.

He could forget about it just now and just mellow in the memory of the taste, and when the memory got dim?

He could just lick his lips again!

He dozed, he came to...slightly...

Then he just fell asleep....

Random thoughts...

Har-ree...

Roll-houses...

Mother and home...

Little Berra brother...

Chee came slightly to his senses when something nudged his hand, just a soft, gentle, tap. His sleepy eyes opened and he looked down to it, he smiled when he seen it, picked it up, and then...

Chee squeezed it, and it gave out a nice little squeak!

His eyes opened wide in terrible realisation!

MAD DOG'S RED BALL!!!

He stood up immediately, and just as he erected himself, he saw the dog sniffing around for its favourite, red, squeaky ball.

Just fifteen feet from him!!

The mad dog turned and saw him.

The dog lifted its head and took a sniff in the air

The beast that it had tried to catch in its back garden!!

IT HOWLED THE MOST EAR-PIERCING, GUT-WRENCHING, NERVE-JANGLING HOWL, THAT EVER A MAD-DOG HAD HOWLED!

THEN IT RAN FOR HIM, SLEVERING AND BARKING INSANELY AS IT BOLTED FORWARD.

THE LITTLE BEAST LOOKED TO THE NEAREST TREE, BUT IT WAS OVER THIRTY YARDS OFF.

THE DOG WAS ALMOST ON HIM!

HE STEPPED BACK IN PANIC AND FOUND HIMSELF COMPLETELY OUT IN THE OPEN, NOW PERFECT BAIT FOR THE DOG WHICH WAS ALMOST READY TO POUNCE ONTO HIM!

He thought he was going to die, there couldn't be any way out of this terrible situation, and as the dog readied to leap onto him, Chee held his arms up and tried to protect himself from the onslaught....

His eyes remained closed and he just stood, waiting for it....

Nothing...

He opened one eye, just a tweak, only to see if he was still alive.

He saw his tormentor, sitting and watching above his head!

Chee looked above himself, and saw the red-rubber ball, still in his hand!

And still being watched by the canine! The dog whimpered in frustration, Chee could see that if he didn't have the ball the dog would tear him to pieces!

Again it whimpered, he wanted to attack, he licked his lips in growing aggression, but every time Chee moved the ball, the dog's eyes had to follow!

He wanted the ball, he needed the ball, he couldn't help himself.

He just had to have the it!

He was a ballaholic!!!

Chee lowered the ball and the dog raised his eyes in expectancy!

The dog's eyes followed the ball wherever Chee took it, if he moved it to the left; the dog would go, if to the right?

So would the dog.

Pretty soon, Chee realised he was safe, but only as long as he retained the ball. Then the mad dog's owner started to whistle, and the dog began to yelp in pure frustration.

Chee lifted the ball, as if to throw it in the direction of

the owner, the dog readied himself, and as the monkey pitched it, the dog hounded off after it.

But Chee still held it, and ran smiling with it to his favourite tree!

He was up the tree and secure, waving down to the mad-dog running around the bottom of, it. It took its owner a full ten minutes and all his strength to pull the beast home, and all the way back it yelled and howled to get its ball back.

And just one more try at the monkey!

Chapter 11

He Says, She Says.

Jill Dunbar watched her husband from the kitchen window at the rear of the house.

She was just ready to leave for work, back shift; she lifted her hat as she walked out to see him. Again he was standing against the fence at the bottom of the garden, he had a pair of binoculars almost attached to his head, and was attempting to scour every square inch of the surrounding countryside, just as he had been doing for the past two days.

She shook her head as she walked toward him.

"George, isn't this becoming a bit of an obsession, darling?"

He didn't take the glasses from his eyes as he continued to spy, and only uttered one word in reply.

"No"...

"It seems to me as though it is"

He only shrugged his shoulders, noncommittally.

"George, look at yourself, look what's happening here, you're convinced that you've seen a monkey!"

Again, he nodded and she continued.

"Here..In Bearsden!"

He continued to view, but swallowed uncomfortably as the suggestion began to hit home.

"And now you think that old Hector what's-his-name has seen it too, I don't think so George"...

She tried not to be insulting with her husband, but she felt that there were certain implications.

"I know what I've seen Jill", for the first time he took

the binoculars from his head.

There was a short delay, and then he spoke.

"To you it sounds completely unlikely, this kind of thing is almost impossible to explain to anyone, never mind someone like yourself..."

She drew her tongue across her lips.

"What does that mean?"

George Dunbar looked into his wifes eyes and earnestly tried to explain the difference in their viewpoints, how both could see it so differently.

"Well Jill, you're a woman"

He had his shovel out, he didn't know it, but he had.

"Mm Mm."

"Well Jill, sometimes, women are ...maybe a little too... practical??"

And he was digging a little hole for himself, not too big to start with ..but...

."You, see things, that make, sense.....you don't see things that don't make sense"...

Jill stared incredibly at her husband

"That doesn't make sense George!

He in turn stared back into her face

"I know it doesn't make sense, that's what I'm trying to tell you!!"

She shook her head now, cause it didn't, then George dug his last spade full of earth.

Maybe he even thought it was his trump card!

"And, after all..." he hesitated slightly...looking downwards at his wives uniform, hat, still in her hand.

"The Police are not known worldwide for their sense of open-mindedness"

This explanation had a quite detrimental effect on

George's argument; in fact, it had almost the entirely opposite effect as was intended.

She duly blew right up at him.

"Oh come on George, not this old chestnut again, you're blaming me! You're blaming my job, for you, seeing a monkey?!"

Then he was in it!

Both feet, right up to his shoulders.

"Tell you what George", she stared dead into his face almost, " This is how much I know your talking through your rear end, you show me a monkey out here, and I'll cancel our trip to Mexico next May and I'll book us all away for a fortnights potholing, remember that one hundred percent brain-dead pastime you used to get up to with your brain-dead brother?!"

He stared back at her, seething, almost shaking with disbelief.

"Well if you come across one, bring it in the house and we'll all have a nice cup of tea together, cos they like little tea parties, don't they, then I, will personally phone and book our dream adventure together in Wales"

He couldn't answer, he was so angry.

"And maybe the monkey can come along with us; he'd probably like that, eh?"

And as they debated the rights and wrongs of it all, the fact that he, a primary school teacher, was convinced beyond any doubt that he had spied a monkey in their garden, and she, a hardened seen it all, done it all, traffic-cop, as far as she was concerned.

It just couldn't happen!

The little beast watched them from high in a densely leafed evergreen, only twenty yards from their home; again his body remained perfectly still, only his eyes moved as he studied the pair of them.

And at that point, he knew he was being watched out for, and hunted...

Chapter 12

Not All as it Seems…

11.15 pm.

"I think old Hectors starting to lose it a little bit John, listen to this"

Hectors neighbour was standing at the back-door and listening to the strange sounds coming from the normally quiet and very straight-laced, old man's garage.

"Do you hear him laughing? He's only in there himself!"

John looked toward the garage and nodded.

"Aye, that's him right enough"

He shook his head quite regretfully.

They could see the garage strip light was on, and could only hear one voice in it, the old mans…

They could see a shadow at the foot of the big double doors; it seemed to be jumping about…

He giggled and laughed, then spoke aloud, as if to someone else.

It soon became clear to both of them; no-one else was there.

They closed the door quietly and retreated upstairs to bed, shaking their heads and muttering sadly to themselves.

"S'pose that's what happens when you get to that age"…

Hector had let himself into his garage, almost trembling with excitement, and after glancing at the flapping window; he was then prepared for anything!

He unlocked, and slowly pulled open the door.

Turned and switched on the light.

His eyes blinked and his heart rose uncontrollably as the fluorescent light flickered in the darkness, and in the few seconds that it took for the light to grow, new images blinked at him in the dark.

Where the monkey had left the last gift!

Then became real.

It was then he shouted her.

"Do you see it?"

He walked toward the small pile, his heart bursting in happiness, and with a grin as wide as the River Clyde!

He leaned down and lifted the pile.

A wiper-blade, a number-plate, a wash-wipe font and a V.W. logo.

Who could believe this?

The old man started to dance around the garage, holding the assortment of car parts high above his head, looking toward the heavens!

Then, speaking to them.

"CAN YOU SEE IT? CAN YOU SEE IT!?"

He skipped and hollered around the concrete floor.

"LOOK AT WHAT HE'S LEFT ME, CAN YOU BELIEVE IT?"

He clenched them tightly, shaking them as he spoke.

"BY GEORGE! LOOK AT WHAT HE'S LEFT ME!"

He stopped and leaned against the workbench, now heaving for breath.

Placing the parts down on the worktop on it, old Hector stepped slowly back.

He looked above himself again, but now spoke a little quietly, thoughtfully.

"What would you make of this little lot?"

A tear trickled down the lines of his old face, as again, he smiled to the heavens.

"My beautiful Elizabeth"...

Chapter 13

Making Up Again.

Six days now since he had made the sighting, and since then?

Nothing.

No monkey, not even a trace of it.

A big, fat, zero.

But the monkey knew where he was, and watched him.

All that he had to show for the sighting was a growing rift between him and Jill, culminating in the biggest row they had ever had, and it was getting no better.

He had brought down her job again; it was almost public knowledge that he had no respect for what she did.

"That old chestnut!" as she had put it.

Things had deteriorated, for the past two days since the slanging match, she had kept out of his way, eating separate meals at separate times, and now she was in a separate bed...

He didn't mind the first night, he was still indignant, still hurt that she could question his sanity.

Him! A schoolteacher!

As if...

So George and Jill both fell asleep that night, each one bristling at the other with the thought of what had been said.

Her job, "They teach you to be cynical; they actually encourage you to be a doubter!"

His mind, "And until I get an apology, you can share a bed with the bloody monkey!"

So on the third day of the forced silence, the stand off,

you can imagine the joy that Jill felt when she finished her work at six-thirty and returned to discover a remorseful husband, a candlelit table, chilled wine and the biggest bouquet of flowers that George could buy!

"A very lucky lady!" remarked the florist, as she packaged them.

And a lovely card to say just how sorry he was, cos he still loved her, and probably more than ever now!

They had the meal and drinks, and both sat on the sofa, holding long and into each other, like long-lost lovers, now eager to make up for the time lost between the two.

"I'm so sorry sweetheart, I should never have brought your job down, I promise never to do it again, I know you love it so much!"

They kissed and held even closer, and then he declared.

"Encouragement, that's the by-word from now on in, I love you and every little thing about you!" he looked over to the patrol cap, sitting on the chair, "I'll even start to love your job, and we'll grow together with it!"

Her face beamed with the loveliest smile.

"Oh, I love you so much George, and I'm sorry about these cruel things I said about you!"

He looked into her eyes, and then smiled into them.

"No, forget that Jill", he looked downward, and slightly embarrassed, "God knows what it was I saw", he smiled as he slowly looked back to her, "or thought I saw!", he shook his head in remorse, "but we're more important than that, it's us that matter from now on in!"...

"I'll drink to that sweetheart!" she agreed, and they did.

Afterwards, they stood in the kitchen, Jill drawing the blinds closed so they could retire for the night. George stood at the door, waiting, and smiling.

Jill turned and spoke as she closed the blinds. "Sweetheart, I love you so much, I never want anything like that to happen to us again, we need to be there for each other, and if you think you ever need to tell me something, anything", she looked into his eyes, clasping his cheeks in her palms.

"Tell me"...

She held into him and they embraced passionately, as if there would be no tomorrow.

He held Jill tighter than ever before and she could feel both their hearts beat as one.

But Jill's heart had started to thud in her chest, to race in her bosom.

For it was then she saw the monkey climb from a tree and enter thick bush, thirty-yards from the rear of their back garden.

She could even have sworn it carried a car registration plate!

"Ermm"...she garbled uncomfortably, hardly able to speak, such was the shock she was in.

She pulled his hand and led him out of the kitchen.

"Let's go upstairs Darling"...

Chapter 14

Prepare to Prepare.

He readied an array of food, so much; it would have been a feast for any monkey.

Peeled and sliced a banana, cored and halved an apple, poured out a good portion of corn flakes and laced them with raisins.

He poured some milk into a bowl, than some water into another.

Then he decided that maybe monkeys like to peel fruit themselves, so he gave another banana and an orange as well, just to keep its brain occupied.

But Hector could see, there was nothing wrong with this wee fella's brain; it was obvious it worked very well.

He lifted the tray of monkey treats and left them on the spot where he had received his gift of honour, an hour earlier that evening.

But while Hector prepared a feast, Jill prepared a plan.

If she never said anything about the sighting, her sighting, maybe it would just go away.

These things are reported all the time, the Beast of Bodmin Moor, and all that, there are always sightings, but no one ever takes them too seriously.

Especially the Police.

At least he was right about that...

The monkey, or whatever it was, will surely wander off in time and lose itself in the same country or forested area that it had sloped in from.

Surely.

George fell asleep, a happy and contented bunny,

drifting off not long after ten, sated in food, drink and love.

He slept like a log, snuggled into his sweetheart, Jill.

But Jill wrestled with her conscience for many hours after that, tossing and turning with the sighting in her mind, almost trying to deny it, and justify her own uncharacteristic behaviour, but every time she tried to close her eyes and drift off.

She saw the monkey, climb from the tree...

Chapter 15

ZanZibar?

Jill left the house at five-thirty next morning to start early shift.

She was absolutely convinced she had only a few hours miserable sleep, her romantic night turned wretched by the sighting at 9.15 the previous evening.

She lay from that time, seeing and hearing only one thing.

The monkey!

The monkey!!

The monkey!!!

She gave her sleeping husband a fretful peck on the cheek before she left, she still hoped what he didn't know, wouldn't hurt him.

My God, she thought, if he found out about this, it could certainly hurt her!

George phoned her at eleven from school, his day was moving along nicely, but he was concerned that she didn't have too good a sleep last night, and was she okay.

She fobbed him off with a complaint about indigestion; maybe she had eaten too much, and a little later than usual. They both agreed that things would be alright by this evening, and finished off by agreeing to have something a bit lighter tonight, maybe a little fish, or salad or something.

Her partner for that week was a rather dull, go-ahead, determined, twenty three year-old male officer, Derek Wilson. Six years younger than her, and very surprisingly for his age, he was a determined and dogged officer, he had ambition and was determined to go as far in the force as he could. This attitude sometimes amused other, more seasoned officers, such as Jill.

"We'll see how long it lasts." was the general stuffy retort, they would nod together, they had all heard this before.

But at this point in his blossoming career, he was quite dogged and remarkably unshakable, and when he thought he could smell it, he chased it.

She tried to engage Derek in some light conversation; they would usually joke, the other, and especially older officers about any Cop TV. show.

They laughingly shot holes in every episode, if only it were possible to detect, investigate and solve all these crimes, in an hour!

Brilliant!

Yet they still watched them.

Unfortunately, Derek never took his eyes or attention off wherever he was, to have much input. Whenever he could spare time for TV. he watched Star Trek, The Next Generation.

Whenever he missed that, it was recorded for him, by his Mother.

So all told, Jill's early morning fairly dragged on, she was relieved as much as she was hungry when lunchtime approached.

The food court at the Supermarket, Jill had prawn mayo and tea, while he got a burger and coke. Jill read the morning newspaper while she ate; Wilson watched the shoppers and slow moving traffic which trundled through the giant car park. He seemed determined not to miss anything, even during his break. Whenever she quoted a snippet from any interesting story, he would generally give a short reply; usually one or two word answers were his norm, his mind was never far from the job.

Both had finished lunch, she had memorized the contents of the paper and they were just ready to drive off. Wilson noticed a patrol car enter the car park, then head toward them.

Jill looked closer toward the approaching car, and then her face broke into an enthusiastic smile.

Brian Sinclair and Fred Walker! She thought, good, I might get a bit of a laugh now.

They sat waiting as the patrol car approached them.

The two cars drew across each other and both drivers lowered their windows.

Sinclair was first to speak, looking over Derek Wilson, toward Jill. As usual he had an ear-to-ear grin set on his face.

"Afternoon Officer Dunbar!" then he looked to is mate, "or should I say Officer Zanzibar?!"

She shook her head and gave both a wry smile.

"Afternoon, and what the hell are you on about?"

Sinclair nodded; eyebrows raised, and then carried cryptically on.

"Zanzibar, well that's where you would get them, isn't it?"

Jill looked firstly to her mate, the solemnly detached Wilson, who never joined in with any mickey taking, and then over across the cars, to Fred Walker, he also smiled broadly.

"What's he on this morning, it's a bit early for the drink, eh?" she nodded dryly toward Sinclair.

"He's on life officer"

"Life!" his partner agreed.

They both continued to grin cheesily, all adding to Jill's complete confusion.

Wilson hadn't taken his eyes off the surrounding car park area as the other three officers joked and scoffed with one another.

Sinclair then went into the glove compartment, and started to slowly hoist a banana up between them.

He began to peel it, all the while, his grin ever widening.

Then his mate started to make "OO, OO" noises.

Just then, Jill felt a dull sensation in the pit of her stomach.

"I think they're making a reference to the monkey"

Jill turned to Wilson; she could feel her face growing redder by the second. He continued to look out of the windscreen as he spoke, quite matter of factly.

"On Saturday past, there was a report made to Bearsden and Milngavie Station, an incident at number nine Leggat Drive"

What remained of the smile just froze on her face.

The two others started "Oo, Ooing" louder as the very serious Wilson spoke, then they started to share the banana, stuffing it in each other's mouths eagerly. She watched dumbly on as Walker then brought out another banana, and started to peel it...

Jill began to feel physically unwell; her voice was barely above a whisper.

"What kind of incident?"

The two others now had their arms raised overhead, fingers outstretched and mimicking monkey-like noises loudly from the other car.

"OO, OO!" "OO, OO!"

"AH, AH!" "AH, AH!"

Wilson continued, straight-faced.

"A wild monkey was reported to have entered number nine", he turned momentarily as he spoke and indicated in Jill's direction with a nod, "That's seven doors down from you", then he stretched his arms and placed his hands on the steering wheel.

The noises still came from the other car.

"OO! OO!", "OO!, OO!"

Then they started to scratch their armpits!

"The animal apparently ran riot through the Muir family's household, completely ransacking the kitchen and bedrooms"

Now she couldn't speak...

She could only whisper as she remembered.

"I was off Saturday"...

She recalled visiting her parents, but by now her mind was a morass of thoughts, situations, sightings and complications, all completely out of her control.

She could only shake her head unknowingly as the other car had by now turned into a gibbering, riotous wall of monkey noises and impressions, the two other officers screeching and hollering, blind to all the traffic which slowly manoeuvred around them.

Wilson did Jill a favour when he started the car then drove off while Walker and Sinclair inspected each other's head.

For fleas…

Chapter 16

What the Public Don't Know…

Mrs. Muir had demanded a visit from an officer, who duly arrived one hour after the incident. He was then flabbergasted to hear the family report to him the events from earlier on that day.

Putting fresh water into the goldfish bowl was the only change to the way the beast had left their home, the officer took note of the disruption in the kitchen, especially the fridge, the assortment of toys, cd's, and many other dislodged articles, which still lay strewn in the rooms upstairs.

But he couldn't believe what he was noting in his little black book, and he suggested that this was probably a grey squirrel that had intruded into their house, "They were known for acts just as this and were recognised as being intrusive and cheeky little beggars!"

This statement cut absolutely no ice with the family of females; they were determined and let him know that, "We chased a beast, a Rhesus Macaque and not a grey, brown or red squirrel, out of our fridge and through each one of the rooms upstairs!"

He had to quickly retract the squirrel theory, the family were so indignant, even the young six year-old protested noisily!

But even though he noted every detail of the alleged incident, and routinely checked the surrounding country area, as far as he was concerned, it could only be, an alleged incident, how could he follow this up? The thought seemed ridiculous to him, there were no other reporting's or sightings of monkeys in this area, and he was sure none would be.

As was W.P.C. Jill Dunbar, but she had seen it, and now tried to convince herself, she hadn't.

As was her husband George, he had seen it first, but his wife was so successful at brainwashing him into believing he hadn't, now he, believed her.

And old Hector Kerr, he had seen it, but he was unlikely to tell anyone at all.

The way he viewed it, he could tell his son Tom, but he was far away, in Liverpool.

His daughter Eileen, even further away in Canada.

But he knew fine well what would be thought if he mentioned on the phone to them from all those miles away, that he had a wee visitor.

Yes, a little monkey, that swaps motorcar accessories for tasty meals just before midnight in his garage every evening!

He would be banged up in an old folk's home quicker than you could get a quick-fit fitter!

Anyway, he didn't want the wee thing to get caught and hauled into a cage, it had obviously escaped from a private collection, or maybe even a laboratory, good luck to him, he hoped the little beast could stay well fed, and hidden.

But in his heart, he guessed it could only be a matter of time before it was spotted, then the place would be overrun with Policemen, R.S.P.C.A. Inspectors, Activist's from the Monkey Protection League.

And probably, David Attenbourgh....

So for now, as far as he was concerned, only he knew of the monkey, and that was the way it was going to stay.

For just now, anyway.

Chapter 17

The Old Red Ball Routine.

Daytime, the back door areas were quiet, work and school took away most of the residents of Leggat Drive during the long daylight hours Monday to Friday, so Chee was sometimes at his busiest and nosiest during these times. The only people at home during the week were mostly housewives and pensioners; consequently, he had pretty much a free reign. He remained hidden to most, the Muir's now thought of him as a transient, they knew he existed but he would probably be far away by this time. He continued to view his kingdom hidden in his favourite tree and came down twice the following day, carefully moving through the copse in search of any scraps he may find. In truth he was now being spoiled, albeit unconsciously by the man, so instead of eating inedible scraps mostly in the daytime, he now waited till night, for his usual, sumptuous banquet in the garage.

The simian didn't take as much care now when he explored. Things had got a little too easy for him, so much so, he knew the mad dog was out most days, and being a kennel dog he knew it was locked in the garden, in a compound.

Strange things were being noticed.

The lady at number 11 stood at her window and watched her dog, the mad dog.

It was barking furiously at something over the wall, racing from end to end, then leaping up and trying to gain access over it

What the devil was Tyson up to?

This was the second morning he'd been this way?

She opened the back door and stood in the frame of it. The dog looked over to her and barked anxiously in her direction. Then his attention was attracted to the other side of the wall and he duly bolted across to it. Again, he barked and pawed madly at the wall, as if wanting to burrow to something on the other side.

She didn't speak, but walked purposely to the wall. The lady slowed as she heard something quite indiscernible.

High-pitched?

She carried on and went to the same side as where Tyson raged at the foot of it. She stood on a rock at the gardens edge, and peered over.

The lady was astonished beyond belief; she could only pull her open hand up to cover her mouth as she stared down, incredulously at the sight of it.

A small, wild monkey, sitting crouched on the other side, looking to the area where it imagined her dog to be.

The dog stopped barking and stared intently at the wall, almost stopping breathing while he listened...

She gasped as the monkey readied itself, and then scurried on all fours to her side. It was completely unaware of her presence above, it looked to the wall on its own level, almost as though it could see through it and could view the dog on the other side!

But if it was possible, she was even more gob-smacked by what it did next!

The monkey pulled up a red ball; she was amazed to see it was Tyson's own, lost, red ball.

It held it up.

Then squeezed it.

Two, distinct times.

Squeak, Squeak.

Tyson came rushing to her feet immediately, then started burrowing at the base of the wall, all the while, barking and howling, almost insanely!

The monkey jumped up and down, seemingly in great joy at the dog's complete and unfettered rage!

On the last jump, it looked up.

And saw her watching it.

In latent and pathetic realisation, the little beast held up the ball toward her.

Almost, apologetically...

Once again, he tried wretchedly to communicate with a human, he uttered a series of chirps and demonstrated a submissive flash of his front teeth, but, in truth, he knew he was caught by a person with the dog's ball.

"I mean you no harm, I'm only a Chee monkey and I respect your area."

Again, translated from the regional Scots Rhesus, to the mortified lady, it sounded like

"AaaaarrrrGGGGHHHHH!!!!"

And after what looked like a threatening show of bared teeth to her, they both ran screaming, her indoors to phone her husband, sister, daughter, son, and anyone else she could think of to tell this incredible story and him to his favourite tree, still with the red ball in his hand.

And soon after that point, at 11.30 a.m., the R.S.P.C.A. became involved.

Chapter 18

Are You Looking for this?

11.20 p.m.

He held three items as he scurried through the bushes to the wall in the early moon glow. A number plate, a wiper blade, and a small piece of plastic trim, torn from the door of a parked car. He had been well accustomed to evening raids in the main road by this time, the streets were virtually deserted after ten-thirty and he found he could more or less skip around the street from car to car, absolutely unnoticed, just as a cat or dog would expect to.

He gripped the plate in his mouth and leapt to the top of the wall behind the old man's hut; he hadn't eaten all day and was more than ready for this meal.

As usual the old man's area was quiet, so he lowered himself quickly then crept toward the garage.

He took one last look around himself before he climbed up to the ledge.

Then he was on it.

After a few attempts, he put the plate in length-ways and then followed it in, ducking under the window in the darkness.

Straight away he noticed there was no food left for him.

He climbed down, and walked in disbelief to the spot where his meal would usually be.

There was nothing there!

He stepped to the spot where it would normally be and inspected it, then slowly lay his three offerings down.

"Are you looking for this youngster?"

He froze as a human voice emerged on the darkness behind him, the soft, slow voice, of the old man.

His body prickled uneasily beneath the thick fur and he could only turn ponderously, almost as if in slow motion. When he turned he could see nothing in the darkness in the area that the voice had come from.

He lifted his head and sniffed the heavy air of the garage to confirm his suspicion.

And in the cacophony of thick, industrious smells, in amongst the fuel and exhaust emissions of the machine beside him, the oils and greases from the cupboards, the metallic tang of all the tooling that permeated the garage air, there was one overriding scent that he had actually noticed, but failed to recognize when he had entered the garage.

He recognized the human scent a little more as he stretched his head toward the sound.

Then the voice in the darkness spoke up again.

"I have food here for you", the simian listened closer in the direction of the sound, then smelled a zip of citrus.

Immediately he salivated.

Then for a moment he thought of the berra tale of food seduction and the She-har.

He hesitated, and then pulled himself back from the darkness, from the unseen, unknown voice.

A segment of orange was then thrown onto the floor, landing on the small shaft of moon glow that shone in through the darkness. Chee looked to it, then to the area that the hand had come from in the corner of the garage. He bent down quickly, not taking his concentrated gaze from the corner and picked it up, stuffing it quickly into his mouth.

The soft, lilting voice continued.

"Nice, isn't it?"

Incredibly, the monkey nodded toward the voice, almost as if in agreement, he stepped forward again, just standing beside the picture of light on the concrete floor.

"Want some more?"

Then a banana appeared. The old man started to sing lightly and move the fruit, as in some kind of little dance, in the half-light in the corner.

"Tum-te-tum-te-tum-te-tum!"

The monkey stared on in the enveloping darkness, all that he could make out was a faint outline of the banana, but fingers held onto it as it touched the shaft of light.

There was a metallic click, then the man's face was partly illuminated. A cigarette lighter glowed just under his chin and for the first time, the monkey could see Hectors smiling face as he sat in the corner. He continued to speak softly with the monkey.

Chee stood watching the man; his face was set uneasily as he stared from the fruit, then to the man, who attempted to entice him with the banana.

"Come on Sonny, you must be really hungry tonight!"

Hector laid the still flickering lighter on the small table beside him, its faint glow lit up the corner of the garage, and then he began to peel the banana.

The macaque grabbed the fruit from his hand then quickly left the garage.

Chapter 19

Pants On Fire.

"Where's the Advertiser Jill?"

"Try the magazine rack!"

"No, I've already tried that"

Jill walked in from the kitchen, and then remembered.

She shook her head in sorrow.

"I'm afraid I dumped it George", she looked toward the kitchen.

"Spilt tea all over it, sorry!"

Liar.

"Oh, right"

"I had to clean the mess from the table, spilt all over it"

He shrugged nonchalantly, "Okay, I'll just check out the TV. bit from the magazine"

"Sorry"...

Pants on fire…

"It's alright, don't worry pet!"

The Bearsden and Milngavie Advertiser was in the bin alright, but it wasn't because of a spilt tea.

Spilled truth?

It contained an article, just a snippet seven lines long.

It read as follows.

Monkey Business.

There was a reported sighting in Bearsden on Thursday last, of a small brown monkey in the country area to the rear of Leggat Drive and Baird Walk.

The stunned resident, Mrs. Shona MacLeod, of 11 Leggat Drive, saw the animal over the wall to the rear of her back garden, before it ran off into a dense copse of trees and bushes which lie nearby. It was less than two feet in height and had thick, brown fur.

The incident was reported to the R.S.P.C.A who in turn, passed on details to Bearsden and Milngavie Police Station.

Chapter 20

A Fair Swap.

Harry Thompson had made no statement that any of his charges had gone missing from the wildlife park. It was quite simple really, in the thirty-five years of the parks existence, nothing like this had ever happened before.

There were no precedents, only rarely were head counts made of the beasts, there were just too many to pin down, to count at any given time.

And up until that point, no-one had noticed that they were one year-old, Chee monkey short.

This was the second sighting of the wild monkey that had been reported to the small Police Station, the report had been passed from the animal charity and they had decided now to act on it, to work in conjunction and get a team of Officers and Inspectors to inspect the surrounding country area, just in case it bit or clawed anyone.

Being the local resident with the best knowledge of the area, a slightly stunned W.P.C. Jill Dunbar was elected to take charge of the mixed force of Police and R.S.P.C.A. Inspectors that were to descend on Leggat Drive at ten a.m. the following morning.

Hector was waiting quietly in the corner when the window was held open and the monkey crept into the garage, at ten past eleven that evening.

Almost as if he wore a watch and could tell the time

A small candle flickered gently at Hectors side.

The monkey looked into the corner, almost as if it expected him to be waiting there.

Hector greeted the macaque, his face breaking into a warm smile while he welcomed him into the candle lit garage.

"Hello Sonny, are you ready for your supper?"

He held out a piece of apple, cored and sliced for the little beast.

The monkey jumped down from the ledge and stood five feet off the man in the corner. He could see there was more food lying beside the flickering candle on the small table by his side.

Hector held the apple slice further forward and spoke again to the simian.

"Well come on then youngster, don't be shy!"

Chee stretched slowly forward and slowly picked the slice of fruit from Hector, and then he lifted his other hand to his mouth and pulled a small object from it.

The little simian then slowly held out the object toward Hector, who sat mystified in the dimness of the garage. He tried to make out what was being offered, and then could see in the flickering light.

A small rubber wash-wipe font, still moist with the monkey saliva.

"Well what's this you've given me tonight then?"

He in turn slowly picked it from the macaque and carefully examined it.

Hector smiled to the little creature that stood before him, watching.

The monkey still held the apple slice in its hand, but when Hector turned from the moulding to speak to the macaque, it looked away and down to the floor, almost submissively.

"My, this is a fine wee wash-wipe you've given me

tonight; I'll put it in with the rest of my collection later!"

The monkey looked up to him, then quickly back down.

"Are you not goin' to eat your fruit?"

Hector lifted another piece, banana this time, and held it toward the monkey.

It slowly picked it from his fingers, but then put its other hand to its mouth again.

He brought out two little tie-wraps, bitten and released from a cars wheel trims, Hector guessed.

"They're the loveliest wee tie-wraps I've ever seen!" he looked to the monkey who still didn't eat the fruit, clenched tightly in his fist.

"Go on then!" he whispered, lifting his open hand to his mouth "Let's see you eat it then!"

He mimicked the eating motion.

Then Chee lifted his fingers to his mouth for the last time, and picked three tiny screws from his tongue and held them out for Hector

"Goodness me!" he exclaimed as he accepted the last of the little beasts offerings.

"One, two three!" again he smiled to it, "Three lovely little screws, they're just beautiful!"

Then the monkey looked into his eyes, and spoke to the man for the first time.

Just a little succession of six chirps and three high vocal utterances.

"I'm only a Chee monkey, but I respect you and your magnificent hut"

Hector was delighted beyond words that the monkey had communicated with him, even though he couldn't understand it, and quickly pulled over another piece of banana.

He indicated the monkey should eat, "Go on now Sonny, eat up!"

The monkey chirped again.

"I thank you for the food, I hope you like my small gifts"

Then he placed the food into his mouth.

Hector lifted more fruit over and held it out for the monkey, and as it accepted it he lightly stroked the skin on the little animals finger.

There were no sounds in the stillness of the garage as the man and monkey touched for the first time, and Hector whispered to it.

"My, you've got very sharp wee fingernails; I bet they come in handy when you're trying to unscrew tiny wee screws!"

The monkey chirped two times, then made a little facial expression, lifting his lips to reveal a row of white, shining teeth.

"I've ran away from my hut and now I'm going home!"

Hector responded to the monkeys utterances

"Yes, and a good wee grip in your fingers", he grasped them a little tighter, and both held and scratched each others fingers, then hands, playfully.

Two chirps, some clamping of jaws, and a few vocal utterances.

"I'm going to sea dance across the sea, to my real home, over water"

Hector fed and played with the little beast for the next hour, and in that time was allowed to pat the creature's fur as it fed. They continued to communicate, Hector mainly told the young macaque that he was a fine and hungry specimen, and Chee praised Hectors hut, as well as him, for feeding him.

And spoke of going home.

Chapter 21

Sonny & Kerr.

10.15 am.

Chee's last day in the small copse of tree's, behind Leggat Drive.

He was startled with the banging and clattering of tools and van-doors in the drive.

Four Police Officers and five R.S.P.C.A. Inspectors had arrived, parking their four vehicles in a line just outside the Muir's home.

Thankfully for the beast, there was no vehicular access to the rear of the buildings, the only way there was a common entrance, about six hundred yards down the road.

Or over the six-foot old stonewall which divided the houses from the common ground behind them.

Chee could feel his heartbeat begin to quicken, the men in uniforms collected in an assembly just at the foot of the Muir's drive, and then opened the rear door of one of the vans.

A cage was taken from the van, and nets were handed to each of the officers.

The simian swallowed hard, food was usually on his mind at this time, but now he had a sickening feeling, almost as if he knew, that he was the subject of a terrible hunt that was just about to start

He moved further into the tree, instinctively trying to find the thickest branches to hide from the men.

Then he turned and noticed the woman who stayed with the cold-water man; this compounded his growing sickly feeling and suspicions.

He looked around the area that had been his home for the last week, biting his thumbnail nervously as he saw them walk the pathway to the house, and then they were out of his sight.

Chee thought fleetingly of his Mother and Berra brother, his heart beat long and slow thuds in his chest.

He waited and watched.

One silent, short minute passed, and the little beast agonised that they would leave the area soon, they surely must.

He must find home.

His eyes screwed in disappointment as the woman officer entered the kitchen and stood at the scene of the incident, the fridge, and the white box.

Then a young girl appeared and indicated where the beast was found to the amazed assembly that was growing in the kitchen.

Then the little monkey could see nothing but uniforms through the window, as officers gathered to view the scene. One or two looked from the window, outside to the back gardens and the little forested area behind.

Chee pulled himself in behind the branches, feeling that, at that moment and from then on in, he was terribly vulnerable and open, and at the mercy of the force that now stood at the back door, and readied themselves to exit.

The men and women walked from the door and assembled in the drying green. The lady spoke aloud and pointed in the direction of the trees and although Chee couldn't understand the words, he was smart enough to suspect what was developing across in the back door area.

The Inspectors from the R.S.P.C.A. were to do a check

in the area for tell-tale signs, trails, paw prints, and excrement.

The four Police Officers were to cross the old stonewall and give the small copse an examination.

Jill spoke to her accompanying Officers, as they were about to climb and cross the wall.

She adopted a slightly ridiculous look as she addressed them, well away from the Inspectors earshot.

"Remember, whatever it was that she thought, she saw in her kitchen", she indicated toward the house with even more ridicule, and then Sinclair gave a faint "oo-oo" noise.

Jill looked back to the assembly of smirking Policemen and carried on, half-smiling herself and continued, "Will more than likely have moved on and away by this time, and if we make enough noise and put up a fair enough show of force", again she sported a playful look, "It will this morning!...."

The male officers attempted to climb the old wall, quite gingerly at first. It was covered in a continual mould of mossy, green lichen, and none of them wanted it on their nice, clean shirts.

Mark Symington, a fit twenty-something, was first over, showing off by almost leaping over with only one hand to balance on, as he hurdled over. Fred Walker was next to attempt it, but he was at least fifteen years older and three stone heavier, so he would do it in two goes, up on the wall first, then jump to the other side. He was crouched awkwardly on top and giggling stupidly as he tried to retain his balance on the slippery surface. He stretched out a hand for Jill, so he could help her up and over.

"I don't need to go over!" she smiled at them, "I'm the

boss today!"

She turned and smiled at Sinclair, who had readied himself to punt her up, he laughed back, still crouching down with his hands cupped.

"Move it Dunbar, if I'm going over, well so the hell are you!"

Wilson gave her a playful shove from the rear. She turned to see him behind her.

"Not much point in asking for any support from you then, eh?"

Something resembling a smile crossed his face as he shook his head.

"Sorry"

Fred Walker was having problems with the slippery, sloping surface of the wall, he grumbled down to her.

"C'mon you, you're the ape hunter supreme, this is your jungle here, move it woman!"

Then Symington moaned from the other side.

"Come on monkey woman, I'm getting hungry, it's nearly time for my breakfast!"

She shouted back over to him, "Have a couple of the monkey's bananas!" then she threw two over to him. Wilson nodded to the other two males at each side of Jill, and then indicated with a nod of his head.

They looked to each other, and then Jill saw them move forward.

They grabbed her and lifted her forcibly up toward Walker, who laughed as he saw her rise to meet him.

"Lift your feet up!"

"I can't, it's slippery!"

"Get her legs Fred!"

"I can't, I'm falling off myself!"

"Well don't fall on us, you fat tub!"

Wilson gave her an awkward last shove on her backside, and then she was up, standing and trying to keep balance with Walker, who was by now, more than hopeless with laughter and no use to anyone.

They laughed aloud as they held onto each other and tried to balance, six feet off the ground on the walls slippery surface.

"And you're going to catch a wild ape?!"

"I told you, I shouldn't be here, I'm the boss today!"

"Yes, let me hold onto your arm!"

He tried to grab; she tried to avoid him.

Then they both literally fell onto Symington.

The R.S.P.C.A. Inspectors had nothing to report.

No leads, no trails, no paw-prints, and no excrement.

They had decided to start at the other end of the street and quietly made their way along the row of houses. They spoke to whoever was in the houses that morning, starting off with a very unsettled Hector Kerr.

This was just what he hoped wouldn't happen.

He watched the Inspectors as they moved and checked around his garden, and he listened to the team of gibbering, jabbering, not too serious Policemen as they searched the country area to the rear.

He hoped that little Sonny was aware that he was being hunted; now he thought; only providence could help him.

The Inspectors left after five fruitless minutes.

Of course Hector hadn't seen it; he hadn't seen anything out of the ordinary in the past week or so.

Of course not.

The last thing in the world that anyone in the search for the monkey expected to see that morning, was a monkey!

Except Jill.

She thought.....

Maybe...but probably...hopefully...

No.

They cracked endless jokes about it, the Beast of Bodmin Moor got it, The Abominable Snowman got it, and Bigfoot got it too!

They had been searching a full three quarters of an hour and everyone knew by this time, Mark Symington had to have his breakfast. By now, Jill was convinced she was in easy street, she didn't quite know how she would explain the search this morning to George, but she had been trained in the art of bluff and slight deception, sometimes it wasn't good for the public to know too much.

So he wouldn't.

And just in case he got word that the teams were doing a search, she had told the R.S.P.C.A. guys that she had checked down her end, and nothing was out of the ordinary,... honest...

Fred Walker had been shouting for Cheeta, waving his net as he called.

Sinclair yelled for Bonzo.

Even Jill giggled when she whispered for Bubbles, Michael Jackson's chimp, as she stood at the foot of a tree!

It was all going remarkably well for a mid-morning stroll in the sun, until Wilson shouted Jill over, to show her what lay at the foot of a poplar tree.

A hubcap and a registration plate.

She picked them up and looked to Wilson, who stood straight-faced, and as usual continued to survey the scene. Then the other officers approached, all still smiling broadly as they picked their way across the overgrown grass and bushes.

Sinclair was first to them.

"What you got there?"

"Dunno, some kids work, by the looks"

Then he continued, studiously, seriously...

"There have been three reports from this area about missing wheel-trims and regi-plates this week"

Everyone turned awkwardly to Wilson, no one was aware of these reports, but they nodded anyway, just as though they were.

"Yes"

"That's right Wilson"

"Mm, Mm"

Sinclair agreed, nodding his head as he spoke, "Doesn't look to have been here too long, right enough"...

"Must be nearly time for my breakfast"...

They all nodded hopefully together, some smirking and dying to laugh, and some just starving...

Fred Walker kicked his foot of the trunk of the tree, to release a muddy deposit from the sole of his shoe.

Then something crackled through the sunlit branches above them, they looked up to see it, hitting off leaf's and stems, then falling lightly at their feet.

A red, rubber ball.

They looked down to it, all in stunned silence.

"There's something up there"

Derek Wilson.

Jill's heart fluttered uncontrollably with these words, she stepped back to look up.

She couldn't see anything; again she tried to convince her colleagues and herself, that there was nothing there.

"No", she shook her head as she tried to catch sight of anything up above, and also convey to the rest that it was nothing, sunlight streamed through the heavy leafed branches, making identifying anything difficult.

"There's nothing there"

They were all looking up by this time; all shading their eyesight from the shafts of dappled sunlight, which stabbed into their eyes.

Then Mark Symington bent down and picked up the red ball.

He squeezed it a few times, throwing it lightly into the air and catching it, while he thought, and examined the sun-drenched branches above.

He then surprised all the others around him, by throwing the ball in the general direction of which it came.

And then everyone was totally gob-smacked to see an arm extend from a hidden place.

And collect the ball.

A short, hairy arm...

Each individual inhaled visibly, palpably, with the sight above them, and the new development.

As usual Wilson was the calmest of any in the situation.

"There it is", he turned to W.P.C. Dunbar, who looked as though she had just seen a ghost.

"There's your monkey up there, straight up, twelve o'clock!"

Then they could all see the beast as he slowly, but carefully, climbed to the upper reaches of the tree, now aware that he was known and vulnerable.

The ball had fallen from its nook in two branches as the Policeman kicked the trunk. He was stricken with horror as he watched it below him, first budge, then roll from its cranny and bounce all the way down and then land beside the force who had gathered in their search for him.

The poor little beast had no notion of why he picked it from mid-air, maybe just a reaction?...

The R.S.P.C.A. Inspectors had been called and were now standing right under the tree. The Police Officers had been delegated to keep a growing band of people, intrigued by the gathering, away from the scene. People hung from their windows with mobile phones attached; some stood watching nosily over the wall.

Jill now knew that her secret was blowing up in her face by the second, and now there looked no way out.

The monkey had climbed as far out as the thin branches would take him, and Mark Symington knew, there would be no breakfast this morning!

At first they had tried to entice the beast down from the tree, with the fruit they had brought, but Symington had eaten most of it.

"Good job it wasn't drugged", remarked Sinclair, rather fed up by this time.

Fred Walker nodded in agreement.

"He would have eaten it anyway"

The macaque climbed further up, the more they tried to entice him, the more the food seduction theory loomed heavily on his mind.

Alas, one of the Inspectors was an experienced tree-climber; he was usually called to rescue distressed cats and such-like, just in this way, but this was a spectacular first, an escaped rhesus macaque. He had the climbing gear attached, spiked boots for purchase, hard hat on, net tucked into his belt, and a loaded tranquilliser dart gun, ketamine, if it had to come to it.

He had a last laugh with them as his colleagues pulled at his harness, making sure it was well secured, and then he started the climb. The moment he started to ascend the tree, Chee looked around for a way out, some kind of emergency escape route.

There seemed none, no other branches seemed close enough.

He noticed the men underneath the tree spread out; they directed the climber when he reached the centre of the tree and by this time, Chee felt almost heartless and sick to his stomach, he knew instinctively he was now being hunted.

Shouts rang out in the clump of trees; they instructed the Inspector to go up, move to his right and follow the monkey. Chee climbed slowly, further up and out, making the thin branches that he rested on bend slightly.

A larger net had been collected from the back of the van and the quickly building crowd of fascinated neighbours spoke in hushed tones as the hunt slowly closed around the macaque.

Then Chee could see the bearded, helmeted man grow ever closer, the man spoke to the animal as he neared, making encouraging, chirping noises, whistling and clicking his tongue as he neared the stricken macaque.

And then, Chee was as far up and out as he could go, the man felt the branch groan with their weight.

Then his experience told him.

If he moved another few inches, this expedition would end.

He lay seven feet from the monkey; they watched each

other intently, staring sharply into each other's eyes.

He stretched out a hand toward the macaque, and then spoke.

"Come on boy, if you don't come down with me I'll need to give you a wee jab"

If it was possible for the monkey to retreat any further, he did, he found it now impossible to swallow, his throat was so bone dry.

"Come on wee man"....

Through the collection of branches and leaves, Chee looked down to the back gardens and could see them packed with people.

Come to see his demise.

Then he could see the man prepare, then point something in his direction.

He opened up his mouth to gulp as he saw the feathered quill of the dart flash, then dig into his arm.

He screamed loudly in pain, the entire collection of humans watching below winced, then watched further, no one taking their eyes from the treetop for a single second.

The macaque pulled the dart from his arm then threw it to the side.

He watched as the man prepared another dart, then he panicked and tried to move back a little further.

His head spun like never before, and he could do nothing as he felt himself slip, then slide from his perch at the end of the branch. The bearded man reached to grab him, but the macaque just slipped from his grasp, and the man yelled to the collection below.

"HE'S FALLING, TRY AND CATCH HIM BEFORE HE-!!!"...

These were the last words Chee heard before he fell

back and off the branch, he then made the same journey down as the red rubber ball, spinning and shunting down the twenty five feet.

He fell against clumps of leaves, was thumped by thick branches and was jabbed by broken stem ends, as he thumped and bumped his way down to ground.

He didn't know how he had done it, but he found himself suspended six feet in the air, holding and dangling from the bottom branch. In his near dream could see uniforms rush to meet him, his nightmare had come true.

Cold-water lady was just about to snare him!

Then, to his absolute horror, she had him, trussed and safe.

It had almost fallen upon her, she who had done all in her power to deny its existence!

Now here it was, safely in her arms; maybe she could make the best of this awkward situation, maybe she could milk it for all it was worth.

She thought of George. She had to tell him something!

"It's alright, keep back, I've got it here!" She moved them all back and looked to have it all under control.

Her colleagues congratulated her, patted her back, and the R.S.P.C.A. boys rushed to get the cage, and she duly stood and milked the situation, yes, she smiled to herself, things might not be too bad after all!

Then the smile froze on her face.

She looked down from her congratulatory stance, with her beaming, flashing smile.

And noticed the monkey baring his teeth, then begin to sink them into her gloved hand!

The pain in her finger became excruciating, as the little

simian bit harder!

Then she dropped the netting and screamed for all she was worth, so loud, everyone in the surrounding streets could hear her!

"AAAAAAARRRRRGGGGHHH!!!"

And while she did that, the macaque broke free from the net, and ran for his life to the bushes!

Everyone watching immediately ran to the old brick wall at the rear and shouted as the mixed team of Police and R.S.P.C.A. guys ran and followed the dazed monkey through the overgrown bushes and grass.

He had survived the tranquiliser dart, he had survived the fall, but could he last much longer?

Unbelievably, his instincts directed him to the last house in the drive, and he struggled to climb the six-foot wall at old Hectors. He heard his pursuers shout behind him when they spotted him lurching from the bushes, then he was on the wall, dizzy and unbalanced, but creeping down to his last resort.

The garage.

The monkeys hunters assembled raggedly at the rear of the old man's back door.

Huffing and puffing, the slightly out of condition officers stood gasping for breath beside the garage.

Two children and one lady stood hanging over the dividing fence, pointing toward the building.

"IT'S IN THERE; IT'S CLIMBED IN AND THROUGH THE WINDOW!!!"

They approached the garage, red-faced and well out of breath.

Derek Wilson being first upon the scene and still fresh enough, took charge. Jill sat against a tree back at the scene of the escape.

A housewife was administering first aid to her bitten hand.

They had tried the old man's back and front doors, but both were locked and unanswered. Wilson walked over to the small window on the garage; amazingly it was closed and locked!

He tried to view inside the small opening, but could see nothing; something seemed to be blocking his view.

Sinclair tried to open the garage side door, but that was also locked.

He looked down as he heaved for breath, and grued at the thick, mossy, green stain from the high dividing wall which was strewn across his and Walkers uniform shirts.

He shook his head as he stepped from the door; Wilson shouted them from the front of the garage.

"Sinclair, Walker, come here quick, the main garage doors unlocked!"

They all gathered, and stood at the front of the garage.

The Policemen, and the R.S.P.C.A. Inspectors.

By this time, the old man's garden was surrounded by about fifty people, the neighbouring windows were festooned with folk talking excitedly through mobile phones, flicking and flashing cameras, and pointing their fingers avidly toward the climax of the chase.

Officers tried manfully to keep them all at bay.

Derek Wilson stood with his hand on the twist grip of the main door, ready to turn, then pull it open.

He turned to check, shooing the rowdy audience quiet.

"We need silence!"

He put his finger to his lips, and held it.

"SSSHHHH!!!"...

And then there was.

Silence...

Everyone watched, and anyone literally, could have heard.

A.

Pin..

Drop....

....

"Net ready?"

The four Inspectors nodded dryly, they stood along the length of the opening of the garage, ready to walk in with the line of net as it tried to escape, and ensnare the beast for good.

Only this time, they were all were wearing thick, protective gloves; all with their jackets on and sleeves rolled down, each one anticipating exactly what had happened to the W.P.C.

Now they were ready for him to bolt the instant the door was swung open; animals can be at their most dangerous within the effects of drugs; so they all knew at this point, just what to expect.

But another stood with the tranquillising gun, just in case...

Wilson waved his hand downward, to quieten any growing whispers...

Still.

Quiet...

He nodded slowly and purposefully, to his colleagues, then slowly...

He began to pull it up ...

And open...

They looked from the ground, and peered into the

growing light of the garage.

They stared into it, unable to comprehend and take in... what it was that they were looking at!

Whaaat???

Hector Kerr sat on the reconditioned Triumph Bantam motor-cycle, wearing an old fashioned round, white crash helmet, thick rounded goggles and dressed in ancient, black-lined racing leathers!

He seemed to give a maniacal smile as he kick started the engine, then it roared spectacularly into life, cascading the garage with a wall of deafening noise and then thick, black smoke!

He gave the stunned Inspectors a crazy thumbs up, then roared past them, ducking down to miss the slide door which was only half-erected!

All the Policemen and R.S.P.C.A. Inspectors were open-mouthed and stunned beyond words or actions as the motor-bike roared past them, and as it did so, the rapturous audience applauded wildly, opening a channel at the bottom of the driveway for it to exit, then speed by!

Then man and macaque, Sonny and Kerr, roared off in the Triumph, and into the streets!

Chapter 22

The Fugitive.

He had a complete two minute start on them, very useful when your astride a 600cc Triumph, and have very good local knowledge, which was the case with Hector. He had stayed in that area since his retiral from the armed forces, twenty years earlier.

It flashed to his mind.

Twenty-five years spent serving Queen and country, and now he was a fugitive!

He laughed aloud at the thought of it, now what would Tom and Eileen think of their stodgy old Dad being on the lam; it was getting crazier by the second.

At least he knew, Elizabeth would be with him on this one, he nodded smiling again to the heavens as he thought about it.

He felt a movement inside the bag behind him, and shouted over the roar of the engine.

"Is that you wakening up Sonny?"

Nothing, the wee soul must be sleeping again!

"You're going to have one sore head after this one, imagine, a hangover at your age!"

He was still beaming when he slowed down to approach the multi-junctioned Kingsway, and stopped for the lights. The old man smiled down to a young, single female motorist, as he pulled up by her side.

He beamed happily, winking as he shouted over the engines clatter.

"Beautiful morning for a drive, Miss!"

She nodded pleasantly back to him.

Then he felt another movement in the bag, and unbelievably, the monkey's head emerged from his rucksack!

The little beast groggily surveyed his surroundings, looking down to the astounded woman who sat open-mouthed, and then retired back inside the rucksack.

Hector grinned and laughed aloud as he watched her stall the car, then he hared off as the lights changed, towards the Clyde Tunnel.

"HA! HA! HA!!"

George Dunbar was rocked, he had tried to contact her at the Station, but she was out.

Then he tried her mobile phone.

It rang for ten seconds, and then she answered.

Jill could see the incoming call was from their house, she winced as she prepared herself.

"Hello."

George was extremely excitable, almost jumping up and down, at the news he had for her.

"Jill, you'll never believe this!"

"I might..."

"Guess who was round at the bottom of the street today?!"

......"Dunno..., tell me...."

"Jill, Scotland Today! and Reporting Scotland!"

Silence

"Are you there? Jill you still there?!"

Silence

"Hello, Jill, can you hear me?"

"Yes...."

"Jill the place was crawling with people from the T.V. and papers!"

He could hardly make out her whispered response.

"Oh my God!"...

"Do you know what it's about Jill?"

She nodded to the phone while she waited in the queue.

"Yes"

"What was it?"

"I'll tell you when I get back"

He hesitated, and then continued.

"Okay, Pet I'll see you later, where are you now?"

Silence...

"Jill, you still there?"

"Yes"

"Where?"

"Gartnavel Royal Infirmary"

"Is it for you? Are you alright?"

She chewed her lip, just before hanging up.

"I'm losing the signal.... George"......

Chapter 23

Is Something Wrong Officer?

"Tango, Romeo one, give me a regi-check on the motor-cyclist we're looking for"

"Roger, Romeo one, its Victor, November, Whisky 447"

He turned to his mate, "That's him right enough Peter"

The patrol car swerved, done a U-turn on the wide street and then raced to catch the green Triumph. They caught up with him in under a minute; the bike was sailing along Mosspark Boulevard at 29.9 miles an hour. The driver watched the approaching Police car in the rear view mirror, the same ones that he had travelled the length of the U.K. to obtain.

They flicked on their blue light, sounded the siren, and then pulled him over.

Hector smiled warmly as the officer walked to him, the officer in turn wondered what this could be about, an all points bulletin for an old age pensioner driving a relic motor bike, and hiding a wild monkey?

"Good morning Officer, how may I help you, I wasn't speeding was I?"

"Would you like to turn off the engine and step away from the bike, Sir?"

He couldn't have been more helpful if he tried, "Yes, yes of course Officer" He pulled the bike up and onto the centre-stand , all the time the other officer was in radio contact with base, the message and accompanying cackle could almost be heard by Hector. The Officer finished the transmission and then walked over. He looked in suspicion to Hectors back as he neared him.

"Are you Hector Kerr, of 25 Leggat Drive, Bearsden?"

He looked around himself, this seemed a total surprise to the pensioner.

Hector nodded eagerly, "Yes, yes I am Officer, is there something wrong?"

"The Patrolman spoke quite awkwardly.

"What do you know about an, escaped monkey",

Hector smiled and interrupted, he seemed slightly incredulous as his eyes twinkled through the round goggles. "I'm sorry Officer; I can't make out what you're saying with this on"

Then he untied the heavy straps of the old style crash-helmet.

The officer looked slowly over to his mate, inhaled deeply, and looked back.

"Sorry Officer I couldn't quite make out what you were asking me there", he tapped the helmet, "With that on it sounded like you were asking me if I knew anything about an escaped monkey!"

Then he stood and laughed at the incredible suggestion.

He stood before the officers, smiling pleasantly.

The officer looked down to his pad, then slightly irritably, back to Hector.

"That's what I did ask you, Sir"

Hector lowered his brows ridiculously and shook his head.

"No I'm sorry Officer, I'm afraid I don't know a thing about escaped monkeys"

"Monkey Sir, singular, just the one", he tried to remain upbeat, but he was aware how absurd the discussion was beginning to appear. It certainly sounded irrational to him, but he continued.

"Can I see inside your back pack"?

"Yes of course Officer". He moved to turn and release the bag, but the Patrolman halted him.

"It's alright, I'll do it"

He lifted the backpack from the older man, and then marched it over to the bonnet of his patrol car.

All the time holding it carefully up and outward.

His mate watched on, looking at the bag and the smiling pensioner in equal measures.

The Policeman unloosened the catch, and then quite warily, he pulled the flap open.

He slowly peered inside, keeping his head well away from the opening.

Then he spoke matter of factly to his mate.

"One Evening Times, one small brown-loaf and one carton of semi-skimmed milk".

He looked painfully toward his mate, walked back to the patrol car, and spoke through the radio.

Hector smiled quite cheerfully to the other Policeman, he in turn, nodded uncomfortably.

The other Officer returned, then asked if Hector could accompany them back to the station, and of course, Hector obliged.

George put on the television as he prepared dinner. The potatoes were simmering and the chicken breasts were grilling along nicely, she shouldn't be long now. The national news had just finished; there was no mention of any murder or anything like that in the area, so he considered it might have been a drugs bust or something

like that to have a TV. presence at Leggat Drive, but he
would know soon anyway, the regional news, Scotland
Today, was just about to start. He smiled excitably at the
telly as he sat at the table, it was just starting.

First headline, the announcer's voice, in low-tones

"Protest at Faslane as nuclear sub is boarded by
launch-borne protesters!"

Then some visuals of the incident.

"Drugs bust," his eyebrows raised in expectation, "In
Clydebank Nursing Home!"

He shook his head and pursed his lips; police cars were
shown outside the nursing home, next one maybe.

"First time lucky for seventeen year-old lottery
winner!"

A little girl was handed a big cheque by Sean Connery.

"Jeez", he thought to himself, "How lucky can
some".....

Then he froze.

"And rogue wild monkey bites Police Officer, causing
havoc in Bearsden!"

He watched on incredulously as his street appeared on
the screen, and a library picture of a Rhesus Macaque was
displayed in the corner.

He felt ultimate, unbelievable release.

Yes!

Then, something else.

YES! YES! YES!!!

Just at that moment, he saw the car appear in the
driveway, and Jill emerge, her right hand newly bandaged.
She had a frowned, and very uneasy look about her as she
saw her husband watch through the window.

Chapter 24

Terry and Gary.

"Terry, that's dinner ready!"

She went back into the kitchen, speaking to her husband in the living room as she passed by.

"Tea's ready sweetheart"

He was in at her back, stealing chips from the plates behind her.

"Hoy! Wait until it's dished!"

He stood on the other side of the table, munching the stolen morsels and smirking in return. Soon after, they walked through to the living room and sat with their plates on their laps.

Mother shouted once more, "Terry, see if that food gets cold!"

Then they heard him trot downstairs, they smiled to each other as he did so. He grabbed the plateful and sped back upstairs with it.

"Thanks Mum!" she shouted hopefully

They heard his door open, and then he shouted downstairs, almost singing his reply.

"Tha-a-anks Mum!"

Terry and Shiela ate their food and watched the national and regional news as usual.

Amongst other items, both were as much intrigued as amused at the story of the little monkey that had been discovered living wild in Bearsden, on the north-side of the city. Possibly an unwanted pet, it was now hunted by Police after biting an officer, an expert spoke worryingly of how dangerous it might be, and what steps should be followed if it was found and cornered.

He and the presenter discussed diseases that could be passed, and how it may eventually have to be shot for the protection of the public.

All, worse case scenarios.

As usual, young Terry sat upstairs eating his dinner at that time, and watched children's programmes

His Mum and Dad didn't see him from five o'clock till almost seven o'clock, when the kids T.V. had finished, every weeknight.

So you could imagine their surprise when he stood at the door at five-forty, straight after his tea, and announced he was going out.

His mother was just about to eat a forkful; she held it inches from her mouth, listening.

Young Terry stood, just his head and shoulders poking inside the door as they spoke to him. First of all she looked at the clock, and then spoke lightly to her son.

"You're going out?"

His voice seemed dry and humourless as he replied.

"Yes"

"Where you going?"

"Gary's"

She looked over to her husband, big Terry, then back to her son.

She was smiling when she asked him.

"You're up to something, what are you going to Gary's for?"

He tapped the schoolbag behind him, then replied glumly, "Homework"

She chewed on her bottom lip as she asked the next question.

"Whose is the bag?" she looked to the back-pack he carried behind him.

"It's Gary's...we've swopped"

"And you just had to have that Adidas bag three weeks ago, and now you just swap it?!"

The youngster shrugged guiltily.

She shook her head and carried on eating as their son raced away toward the front door.

"BACK FOR EIGHT!"

"Okay Dad"

While they ate, Mother thought, and with each mouthful, she thought more.

"He's up to something Terry.

"No..."

"Telling you, this was what he was like that time they started smoking", she pointed her fork at him, "Remember?"

Then big Terry became reflective and replied quite dolefully, "I had a good go at him Sheila, I don't think he would ever try that again"

"Well if he's hanging about with that Gary one, anything's possible"

"And what if they're just doing their homework right enough?"

"Yeah, and pigs might fly..."

Terry Connolly positively rushed to the park, and throughout the fifteen-minute journey, he did act suspiciously. He had muted, whispered conversations, as if to himself, and when he arrived, he ran straight for the dense thickets of tree's and shrubbery, which lay at the parks south side.

Then he melted into it.

A meandering footpath wandered through the brush, a tree covered walkway, but he chose to enter the dense canopy at its thickest, most impenetrable region.

He walked for another ten minutes or so, and eventually arrived at their favourite hidden spot, a scenic and secluded, dell, a clearing of just forty square yards or so, where the sun seemed to burst through the canopy above and shower wonderfully onto the little spot.

A small rivulet gurgled through, where at its widest and shallowest point, Terry and his pals would sometimes try and guddle any small fish that swept by, almost always without success.

Once he was into it, he stopped and gave the surrounding greenery a good examination. Then when he was satisfied that he was alone, and only then, he released his bag.

All the time, he whispered mutedly, almost as if to himself. As he untied the top of the satchel he spoke consciously towards it.

"I'll let you out for the toilet, but I'll need to put a strap onto you in case you run away, your still not right"

He opened the flap, rummaged about for a few moments, and stretched inside it.

Then he pulled out Chee, and clumsily placed him on a patch of long, thin grass.

It was quite obvious the little animal was still recovering from his earlier stupor; he sat for some time and looked around himself. He swayed from side to side and struggled to stand up whenever the youngster re-assured him.

All the while, young Terry held onto a dog extension lead, which was strapped around Chee's neck and offered continual encouragement to him.

The ten year-old constantly watched and listened around as he tried to walk the monkey.

"Come on Sonny, do something, you've just had some dinner, do it!"

He froze when he heard movement coming through the brush toward him, then he rushed to pick up the monkey and stuffed him; still half groggily, back into the bag.

He stood in front of the bag in the small clearing as the sounds came close and became more apparent.

Terry looked down to his wrist; the lead was still connected and led from his arm to inside the backpack. He shook it quickly free, stuffed it inside, and then stood back in front of the bag.

A twig crunched, he looked quickly over to his right. He stared into the brush, but could see nothing.

He started whispering again, only this time it was a nervous spasm, his chin had started to judder.

"HE...HELLO?"

Then there was a crunching over to his left, again his head swept over in the direction of the mysterious noise, was there more than one of them?

"WHO'S THERE?"

There was no noise, except the little lad's heavy breathing as he spoke through the small clearing, but then he watched as a stone was thrown and landed behind him, making more suspicious noises.

He shook his head in relief; he was aware who was behind all this now. He shouted in relief to the culprit.

"ADAMSON, YOUR NOTHING BUT A PLONKER, COME OUT I KNOW ITS YOU!"

Then he saw another stone fall to his left, and he could see where it had come from, an arm was quickly pulled back into a thickly flowered bush.

"There you are, over there!" he pointed to the exact location, and then waited hands on hips for Adamson to appear.

Gary Adamson skulked forward and crept toward his pal.

Terry gave a quick glance behind himself and down to the bag, relieved the monkey was quiet.

He urged his friend forward, eager to confide with him

"Hurry up Gary! Quick!" Terry still looked around the glade, just in case.

"I've something to tell you, something to show you.

Gary Adamson stood before him, and as usual, had a worldly smirk on his face. The same age as Terry, ten years old, they had known each other since nursery school, and at most times to his Mothers regret, he had been Terry's best pal through these years. Terry looked toward Gary in dead earnest.

"See what I tell you Gary" He bit his lip anxiously, "See whatever I say to you and show you"

"Yeah, right!", then Gary mimicked his pal.

"See whatever I show you and tell you"....

As usual, Gary was quite dry. He thought, even at ten years of age, that he had seen it all before.

"What is it this time, have you found money, or what?'

"Gary!" Terry looked down toward the bag, and gave a pointed look to his pal.

Gary nodded, and relented.

"Alright ", then he went into the practiced spiel.

"I, Gary Adamson, of 28 Torscrags Road, promise

never to say to any person living", Terry nodded him on and Gary grudgingly continued, "Anything said or shown to me by Terry Connolly"

"Finish it!"

"I swear "...

"Go on!

"I swear, I'll tell no one your secret!"

"And?"

Gary nodded, licking his lips in thought, and continued.

"I swear and promise that if I do tell anyone, I will turn overnight and without my knowledge, in my sleep, into the world's biggest Celtic Fan!"

Then he made a noise of great revulsion at the thought of it.

"Yeugcchh!!"

All the time, Terry made sure Gary didn't cross his fingers.

The two lads sat down beside the bag while Gary slipped his socks and shoes on.

"On the way back from my Aunties today?" Terry was watched every day just after school by his Aunt and Uncle, until his Mum had finished her work.

Gary nodded.

"I was cutting through here, the short-cut?" he nodded through the woodland to the gnarled walkway used by the public, "And, you know the metal chair?" Gary nodded, still trying to show some interest. "Then I found this", he nudged the bag with his foot. Terry slipped his hand from his jacket pocket, then released and opened a small hand-written note.

"What is it, somebody's shopping list?" he drawled.

Terry drew his pal daggers, told him to "Shoosh!" then turned from him and continued.

He peered into it, and then started to read the note slowly and methodically, written in old Hectors long-handed and rather old-fashioned style.

"Please help me, I am a free spirit"

"Was it somebodies bottle of whisky?"

Terry turned and leered to Gary again, "I'm trying to read this to you, will you shut up?!"

Gary just shrugged as if he couldn't care less, looked back to the mysterious backpack, and then poked it with his outstretched fore-finger. Terry in turn pushed him off.

""Keep your hands off till I read this!"

"Hurry up then, I'm dying of boredom!"

Terry shook his head annoyingly, and then turned back to the note.

"Please don't contact either the Police or the R.S.P.C.A. if you are the one to find me, because they are hunting me"

"What is it, a bank robbing duck?"

Terry clicked his tongue in despair.

"I have been shot by a tranquilliser dart and in the process I bit a Police woman when I tried to escape and am now being hunted"

"OH NO! IT'S A SABRE-TOOTHED RABBIT!"

Terry shook his head pathetically, and tried to carry on.

"I am still very sleepy and groggy, so let me rest till I awake, I'm really quite kind and friendly and if you know me long enough, I will exchange gifts with you"

Terry took a last, serious look toward Gary.

"P.S., my name is Sonny and I love tangerines and bananas"

Terry's heart was thumping as he finished the note; his breathing was long and heavy as he looked from it to his best pal.

"Tell no one Gary!"

Gary nodded, and looked again, smiling to the bag.

Then it moved, they could both see it physically roll over a little, just then the impish expression began to slip from Gary's face.

Terry smiled supremely, and then spoke toward the bag,

"Are you awake yet?"

The two boys watched, with Gary's jaw dropping lower with every second that drew past, as one, then two, long brown fingers crept from the dark recess of the bag and lifted the flap.

For the first time in his young life, Gary was stunned into complete silence, and absolutely lost for any word as Chee, or Sonny, slowly climbed from the bag.

Terry laughed so much at Gary's amazed reaction, he thought he might die!

Chapter 25

Going Pot-holing.

The word was officially out; a brown rhesus macaque monkey had been living wild in the little acre of forest, just to the rear of Leggat drive in Bearsden.

Strathclyde Police had an ongoing investigation with the R.S.P.C.A. into its current whereabouts', and George Dunbar had pre-booked his annual holiday.

Not the mega-trip to Mexico, but a fortnight's potholing in Wales. He was going to be accompanied by his potholing-mad brother Gerard and his like -minded wife Arlene, plus of course, the lovely, if a little scheming, but sadly thwarted, Jill.

The four were to stay in a small static caravan, the same one used by George and Gerard in their single days.

Gerard and Arlene apparently couldn't wait!

News of the macaque's appearance, then disappearance, had been reported on local evening news programs, and both were watched by the absolutely gob-smacked George.

He recorded the second one for smug posterity, and, it was also reported in the daily Nationals.

Copies of these were also retained.

The only person volunteered for an interview after the event, was the tree-climbing Inspector Tom Brand, he was the one who seen it up closest, testified to the animals identity, and yes, definitely a Rhesus Macaque.

Oddly enough, the Police officer in charge of the morning's hunt, the one bitten by the beast, was strangely unavailable to the many reporters that early afternoon; she would have been much lauded on the national TV. and newspapers, but for her own, obvious reasons, she declined.

Chee's remarkable appearance was even given a six-line paragraph in the one of the biggest selling daily newspapers in the U.K.

Terry and Gary stayed with the slowly sobering little beast till nine o'clock, stroking it and just getting lost in the incredible moment of finding a lost monkey in a back-pack!

Then Terry was suddenly aware of the time.

He was to be in by eight!

Both boys split up at the end of Torscrags road, little Gary pushed his hand into the backpack, and gave the monkeys head a tender tweak and wished it a good night. Neither of the boys had any inkling of the little beast's gathering notoriety, or of its appearances on regional television and newspapers.

Both then made their way home determined to tell no one, although both were bursting to.

Straight in the house, then straight upstairs, his mother looked over to his dad from the newspaper.

"That's him in now, an hour late!".... She looked up at the wall clock, very straight-faced.

Luckily for little Terry, his Dad responded first.

"I'll go up and see him"

The youngster heard the footsteps on the stairs, and then he stretched over and tied the straps up on the bag. He approached the door and stood at it as his father neared.

He opened it and stood by as his Dad walked over.

"Where were you till this time?"

"Sorry Dad, we just went down to the park and ended up playing football"

His Father tried to remain serious, but he did think his wife was overreacting.

"Do you promise me?"

"Yes Dad"

Little Terry stood with both arms at his side, and crossed both sets of fingers as he lied uncomfortably to his dad.

Dad nodded, then ran his fingers through his son's hair, "Don't kid us on son, you know your mum thinks you're up to something, she worries about you all the time"

He could feel his face starting to beam slightly, and then he bit his lip and crossed his toes also for this one.

"I promise you Dad, we're not up to anything";

Honest Dad, this is not a bad thing we're doing, I just can't tell anyone...

Dad looked down to his angelic little son, and of course believed him. He nodded and told him to get washed up and come down for his supper.

Big Terry started to walk downstairs, and then his son spoke.

"I'm not hungry Dad...I'll probably just stay up here and go to my bed"

He stopped in thought, but never turned on the stairs.

He felt slightly deflated, maybe there was something after all? He nodded then continued.

Big Terry said nothing of any growing suspicions that he may harbour to his already extremely dubious wife.

At nine thirty-five, Terry's Mother called him down to the phone, it was Gary.

He was sure that Sonny would be okay under the bed,

still secured in the bag.

"Terry it's me"

"What is it?"

"Are you going to School tomorrow?"

He looked from the hall into the living room, where his parents watched TV. then he spoke with his hands covering the phone.

"Supposed to be", he whispered.

"Yeah, so am I" then he whispered, "Supposed to be"

Terry's mother walked from the living room, her son's eyes followed her suspiciously as she climbed the stairs.

He whispered to his pal, "Need to go, see you tomorrow" and then he flung down the phone. He could only watch on helplessly as she turned right at the top of the stairs, she must be going in to my room!

She had her hand on the handle and was just ready to turn it open.....

Sheila heard the crashing; the human crumpling noise in the hall, then her son's cries rang out, piercing into the hallway. Immediately his father was standing over him, looking down at him as he held onto his ankle. He looked down to his painful foot, but all the time he could see his mother in his peripheral vision at the top of the stairs looking down at him.

"What did you do?" she spoke in a scolding manner, rather if she was suspicious after all.

"I fell and tripped on the step", he continued to bleat and moan with pain as his father soothed the inflamed tendon.

"I think he's sprained it, is it sore?" Young Terry nodded pathetically.

Then his Mother pointed accusingly to the trainer that

lay by his side. She wasn't quite as sympathetic as his Dad. She pointed accusingly.

"How many times do I have to tell you to tie your shoelaces!?" she bellowed, "This is what happens when you ponce about posing with your laces just tucked in!"

Dad continued to rub the ankle reassuringly and smile, he tried to speak to his mother, but as he turned upward, he found he couldn't speak,

The monkey walked slowly behind his mother, then stopped just out of her sight behind her. It looked down to see him sitting at the foot of the steps, dazed and absolutely dumbly astonished at what he saw upstairs. He continued to moan, trying to divert both his parents attention, then it lurched around the corner and padded out of his sight

From there, he knew it was headed in the direction of his Mother and Fathers bedroom!

Young Terry gave out another enormous moan, keeping their visions directly downstairs, and on him.

"AAAAHHHH!!!!"

Amazingly his dad was still looking to the sore ankle, still soothing and trying to alleviate the pain by rubbing the ankle, "How's that son, any better?" little Terry stared dumbfoundedly back to his Mother, who now walked slowly downstairs, looking strangely sympathetic!

"He's gone a funny colour Terry"

His dad picked him up and carried him through to the sitting room,

And yes, he had gone a very funny colour, his pallor had changed in seconds, now he was pale and sweating, his mother dabbed his cheek with a damp cloth as he sat up in the settee. Both parents were now concerned and watched over him.

The youngster stared toward the door, convinced now that it was just a matter of time before his unknown guest, the monkey, would come staggering through it.

His Mother would go through the roof!!!

He just waited helplessly, listening and waiting for it, for any sound whatsoever from the upstairs, My God, he thought, it's in their room , it can only be a matter of time before it comes crashing down the stairs, just as he pretended to!

His parents attended him, reassuring and encouraging, then after five minutes or so, he decided he had to get back upstairs, before any of them did.

"I think I'm alright now Mum"

"Are you sure, you don't look too much better"

He nodded, "No, I am, I'll just go up to the toilet and get washed"

He knew he would be unescorted if he was going up to the toilet.

"You go up to the toilet and get washed up for your bed, you'll feel better after that wee man and we'll come and see you before we go to bed", she was all smiles and cuddles now.

"Okay wee man?"

She rubbed his head and then he walked to the door, with only a thin smile on his lips.

"Right Mum"...

He consciously closed the door behind him, then warily, and very scarily, he climbed the stairs.

He crept to the top of the steps and glanced down toward them, he knew if he was found in his parents room, there would be more questions, he bit his lip and went in anyway.

The door was slightly ajar when he reached it, and when he opened it, it creaked and squeaked, and that made him wince all the more!

Little Terry whispered and clicked his tongue to the little monkey as his head turned round the door.

He prayed to himself he would find it, maybe he was sitting in front of his Mothers mirror, wondering who the heck that was sitting in front of him.

He was shattered when he saw the room was empty, he ran to the wardrobe, looked inside and around it, nothing, he looked around his Dads computer workstation, still, nothing!

He ran toward the spare room, at the same side as his room, but that room's door was closed. He walked without any hope at all to his own room, but just as he went to walk in, he had a terrible, sobering thought.

UNDER HIS MUM AND DADS BED, OH NO!!

He rushed straight to their room and threw himself to the side of the double bed. He pulled out a dusty assortment of suitcases, bags, magazines and books, but alas, no monkey! He stuffed everything back when he heard the living room door open, and then swept quietly across the top landing while his parents switched off the lamps and TV. He noticed the bag on the middle of his bedroom lay open and empty, from that moment, that was how his heart felt. He looked to the window, it was swung open and the curtains flapped loosely in the light wind. He tried to speak, but could only whisper one word, his new pet monkey's name.

"Sonny!"....

He stood at the window, two floors up, with his body

drooped over the sill, trying to catch some sight of it around the back door, but he couldn't.

He called a little louder for it but there were no signs of any life, bar some birds settling down to roost for the night in the surrounding rooftops.

"Are you goin' to bed son?"

He slipped back down, and then turned dejectedly to bed.

"Yes Dad"...

His Daddy tucked him in, pecked his cheek and wished him a good night.

Little Terry returned, and spent the next hour at the window, with moist eyes peering hopelessly through the glass while he repeated his message over and over again, his voice just about breaking with emotion.

"Where are you Sonny? Please come back"

When he could stand the chill no longer, when the moon was cloaked by cloud and complete silence, he turned to his bed.

A rumble awakened him, daylight; his Dad was leaving for work. He checked the clock through weary, sleep-encrusted eyes.

6.15 a.m.

He knew that he hadn't slept for most of the night; only a few hours miserable sleep...

Watching all night, listening out for him.

He looked through narrow slits toward the window, light was streaming in the open curtain and it burned into his tender vision.

The window was closed, but he had left it open!

Terry sat up slowly, and as he did, he felt a movement beside him.

He slowly turned around and was amazed beyond words at what he saw!

The monkey lying in the other side of the bed from him, tucked in even!

Terry's face broke into the widest grin imaginable, he came too immediately, and his heart pounded with immense happiness.

He was back! His little friend had returned!

His heart soared with complete happiness, now he knew; today was going to be the best of days!

Chapter 26

A Day to Remember.

Sheila walked downstairs thinking to herself.

Hundred things to do today, need to get these standing orders sorted out, got to get the road tax for the car, the final payment for little Terry's school trip to Amsterdam.

She opened the living room door and stood under it, completely lost for words.

Little Terry was sitting, washed, dressed and ready for school.

And he had the warmest, glowing smile she could remember.

She looked quickly toward the clock, she must have slept in!

7.10.??

"Morning Mum!"

She wet her lips, and then inhaled deeply.

This had never happened before.

"Morning, what's happening here, what are you up at this time for?"

He just smiled genuinely and shook his head.

"Dunno Mum", he shrugged, "I've been awake since Dad left at six this morning, must have been getting to bed early last night, but I'm not tired at all now!"

Her eyebrows started to come down, then meet.

"You been fed?"

He kind of sung his reply.

"Yeah, had cocoa-pops and toast"

Something's not right here...

He stood up and lifted his jacket.

"I'm going to go now Mum, see you at five?"

Sheila looked to check the weather, dry, and just a little cloud in the horizon.

She nodded straight-faced to him.

She knew something was up, from this point in, he was going to be watched, especially with the weekend coming up. She walked him to the door.

"Right wee man, I'll see you later", then she smiled at him, "Maybe get fish and chips tonight, a good start to the weekend, eh?"

"That'll be great Mum!"

He stretched up and gave her the kiss she always got, just before the front door was opened and anyone could see them.

Especially Gary, he would never live it down.

"Bye Mum"

"Bye Pet"...

Then she noticed something creep across his eyes, the innocent, angelic look, just kind of washed off, he never looked to her as he spoke.

"Nearly forgot my bag, I've left it upstairs!"

She watched him as he ran up. The pleasurable look was now washed off her face, she cupped her chin in her hand while she considered.

I'm going through his room tonight, and if I find anything....If I find one little thing....

He was in his room for longer than she expected, and when he appeared, the bag, Gary Adamson's bag, was fixed and strapped on.

She was sure they mostly just slung the back-packs over their shoulders; now this one lay kind of heavier than usual...

What???

Luckily for him, the phone rang.

Little Terry sneaked downstairs while his Mum spoke to his Dad.

"Bye! See You!!!"

He beamed as he walked stridently down to the park, it was too early for any of his school mates to see him, no one would have seen him leaving the house, he would just be marked down as off, and sick.

Happens all the time, there's always someone sick!!

Gary had been there a full ten minutes before Terry had even left the house, he threw a withered branch into the trees in hopeful anticipation, he surely understood what he had meant!

He walked to the rivulet; bit his lip while he stood looking into it, then inhaled heavily.

The little guy looked to the spot where they always entered the glade, and stared into it.

Surely he'll come; they've got to come!

Watching little guppies swim along.

Wonder if they're going to guppy school?

Or going absent, just like me?

He looked to his watch again, if he doesn't come in the next ten minutes, I'll need to start heading to school!

Ach!

He thought he heard a shout from the surrounding forest; he looked up, and listened keenly. His eyes scanned the darkened trees and bushes, he lifted his hand to screen and protect his eyes from the growing sun.

Then he heard it again!

He looked closer, and peered into the area that the sound, the shout, had come from.

Then he saw movement!

And in the greenery that enveloped him, through the overgrown grass, bushes and shaded stems of the forest, he watched the movement become closer and clearer.

His heart soared when he could make it out! Once again, a very easy smile was set in young Gary's face, Terry was walking through the under growth and the little monkey, Sonny, was by his side. As they neared he could see they held hands, Terry stepping over logs and withered branches, while the 'wee man' leapt up, then down, all the while supported by his young masters hand.

"Morning Ape-man!"

Terry shouted back from within the confines.

"MORNING!"

They broke through the clearing and Gary bent over, doubled up on his knees.

Then he pulled out a little tangerine from his pocket and held it out invitingly.

"Come on over wee man and let's see you!"

The wee man let go of Terry's hand right away and walked over. Gary could see a dog bungee chord attached to a collar around the monkey's neck.

He gently picked the fruit from the boy's hand, then he jabbed his front teeth into it and started to peel it.

"Did you have any problems when you went home with him last night?"

Terry's face screwed unbelievably as he answered.

"Did I have any problems? I'm surprised you didn't read about it in the papers!"

Both boys were totally unaware that the monkey had actually been in the papers, and on the television!

"What?"

He sat down and continued.

"When I was on the phone to you?"

"Yeah?"

"My Mammy was upstairs shouting at me cause I kidded on I fell downstairs, cos I thought she was going into my room and find Sonny!"

They both looked to the macaque, munching industriously.

"Yeah?"

"Then I saw him!" he pointed to Sonny, "Walking past her, then into her room!"

"No!"

"Yeah!!!"

They both looked at Sonny as he munched the tangerine.

"Did she see him?"

"No!" Terry shook his head thankfully, Gary looked down to the simian and rubbed his head, "Boy, you're crazy wee man, that was crazy!"

Chee looked up unknowingly while they praised him; he pulled some seeds from his lips as he ate, and then handed each seed, singularly to Terry, who smiled as proud and as pleased as punch as he did so.

"I don't know why he does that", he smiled, "I just stick them in my pocket anyway, we might grow a tangerine tree when we get back!"

He nodded, continued to beam happily, and placed them in his jacket pocket.

"I don't know why"...

Gary smiled over, "What happened after that?"

Terry gulped, "You won't believe me Gary, but I swear it's true!"

"What?" his eyes were as wide as an owl's as he listened.

"After that, I couldn't find him; he must have got out my window!"

Gary shook his head in disbelief.

"What?"

"I swear to you, he opened the window himself and climbed down the two flights!"

"Jeezo!"

"Yeah!", then he thought for a second.

"Either that or he climbed up on the roof!"...He whispered, almost to himself, "And I spent half the night looking out of the window until I was shivering and then I had to go to bed, thinking I wouldn't see him again!"

They were both looking and petting the little beast as Terry explained the unlikely scene, then Terry's eyes screwed ridiculously at this point.

"I must have fallen asleep at five o'clock or something, but then I was wakened by my Dad going to work at six"

Gary sat transfixed, hardly breathing while he listened.

"Yeah"...he whispered.

"And I turned round, and this one's lying in beside me!"

They both looked from one another to the monkey.

"Under the quilt even!!"

Gary couldn't hold back and from then on in, giggled uncontrollably for the next full minute, imagining in his mind's eye, anyone wakening up in the morning, with a monkey lying beside them!!

He lay down laughing; he rolled over laughing, so much so, Sonny stepped back in uncertainty.

"I suppose he even had your jammies on too, ahhh, ha,

haa, haaaaaaaaa!!!"

Chee stood well away till the hilarity had stopped, and it didn't for quite a while, they kept falling back into it, reminding themselves of the ridiculous scene and giggling insanely with each other over it.

A monkey, in bed, with someone's jammies on!!!!

Then, when the laughter had stopped a little and they had quietened a bit, they planned for breakfast.

"Talk about two great minds thinking alike?"

The two boys had the contents of their bags laid out and had started to examine the contents for a breakfast inspection. Terry had managed to get four bananas and three oranges out of his house, Adam had just bought two bananas, a small bag of tangerines, and had taken his Mums pack of dates from the fridge. All the fruit was for Sonny, he seemed to be their first, and in Gary's case, his only priority.

It was just about then he realized that he had no food.

He asked Terry pointedly, "What did you get for yourself?"

Terry pulled out a paper bag and began to empty it.

Gary watched with growing attention as his friend carried on.

"I made this when my Mammy was still asleep at quarter past seven, its the first time I've ever made it", he looked from the uneven cut bread, stained around the edges with red and brown colours to Gary, "My Mammy usually makes my packed lunch"

Gary looked quite disgusted, he pointed to the bread.

"What's that supposed to be?"

"Peanut butter and jam sandwiches"

Gary grued at the mention, "Oh no! That sounds vile!"

Terry looked back, quite annoyed, "Nobodies forcing you to eat it, Nobodies even asking", then something clicked in his mind, making sense to him for the first time.

"As my Mammy says, hunger's good kitchen!"

Gary looked back, completely confused.

Now, the old saying made perfect sense to Terry, he had been told that since he was an infant. He nodded as the message hit home.

"In other words, if you're hungry enough, you'll eat it!"

Gary could only watch on with the same horrified expression as seconds before.

"You'd need to be dying of starvation!"

Terry shrugged noncommittally, he can suit himself.....

He held up a can of cola, then he rustled in the bottom of his bag and brought out the remnants of a packet of penguin biscuits, just two left in the pack. Gary bit his lip looking at the biscuits.

"Can I have one of them?" he pointed hopefully to them. Terry nodded back after a quick think about it.

"Yeah" he threw one at him. All the time that the boys unpacked, the monkey watched on. He had been given a banana and had peeled it and chewed along as they discussed their breakfast.

Gary tore the paper off the biscuit and ate it hungrily, he had been up for nearly two hours now and this was his first food in that time. Earlier he couldn't think of it, now the thought was consuming him. Watching Gary eat made Terry think about it, so he sat down beside Chee and started to prepare himself. He joked with the monkey as he started to eat.

"How's your breakfast Sonny?"

Sonny stopped eating as he watched Terry sit down

and feed himself, as with humans, this little simian thought someone else's food always looked much tastier than his own.

Terry bit a mouthful and smiled at him as he ate, "You wouldn't like this Sonny, its bread and peanut butter!"

"And jam"...complained Gary

But both boys smiled as the little macaque laid down the banana and raised himself.

Then he stretched out toward Terry's peanut butter and jam sandwich.

Terry turned to Gary, and then to the food he was holding inches from Sonny's grasp.

They both wore confused smiles.

"Do you think I should give him a bit?"

Gary lifted his eyelids, "Why not? If you like it a monkey's bound to"

Terry shook his head, "I might act like one, but at least I don't look like one"

He smiled then broke off a corner of the sandwich and handed it to Sonny.

The little monkey sniffed it, and then chewed it slowly. The boys were highly amused by the animal's antics, his ridged eyebrows came down and met to just above his eyes, giving the impression of a rather serious little individual at this point, which of course as the boys knew was not the case. When the sweet taste of the jam and the nutty flavouring of the peanut butter attacked his taste buds, he lifted the ridge of brow in gathering appreciation.

He swallowed and then held his hand out for more.

Both boys laughed at the thought, but Chee was now getting quite insistent, he wanted the rest of the sandwich.

"Do you like that Sonny?" Terry sat fascinated and

completely gave in to the little monkey.

It stood over them and gorged himself on the sandwich, completely savouring the new taste.

"I think he's going to want your other sandwich!" laughed Gary, "He looks as though he loves it!"

Terry held the other piece of bread in his left hand, and tried to shield it from the monkey's vision, but it was futile. Chee knew there was more and bent across Terry to eke out the last delicious slice.

"No Sonny, that's my breakfast, lunch and play-piece all together" he protested "go and have a banana!"

The monkey wouldn't give him any peace and stretched further over to Terry's side, he knew there was another bit. This tickled Gary pink, he laughed as Terry complained

"Look Sonny, this is what you're supposed to like!" He held a banana in one hand, and then inserted the sandwich into his mouth and out of the monkey's reach, while trying to recite from old Hectors hand written note, which he held in the other hand.

"P.S., My name is Sonny" he blurted through the bread, "I love tangerines!" he pointed to one "And banana's!"

Gary giggled as the monkey tried to stretch up.

While Terry was trying to show the monkey a banana, Chee leapt up and pulled the sandwich from his mouth. It scurried off, as far as the extension lead would allow, and sat eating with his back turned to the boys.

"Jeez, that was my lunch"......

"Ah, stop carping on, the wee man's hungry, you can see he's never had a peanut butter and jam sandwich before" then Gary laughed "Obviously he was impressed by your taste in food!"

Terry just smiled and inhaled patiently.

"At least I've got my Penguin biscuit and can of coke!"

He looked horrified as the monkey turned to look when he heard the rustling of the biscuit being unwrapped.

Chee pushed the last bit of the bread into his mouth, then still chewing, rose to investigate the new taste sensation, another first, chocolate.

Terry was wide-eyed and mimicking fright as the monkey walked over to him.

"Oh no, your surely going to leave me something for myself!"

He chewed on a mouthful, but could only smile warmly down to the monkeys inquisitive gaze.

"You want to try this?"

Chee picked it from his grasp and licked the chocolate bar. Both boys smiled broadly.

"Tasty, isn't it?"

Chee seemed to agree with Gary, and then he bit into the biscuit, crunching the bar messily into his mouth.

"Penguin!" explained Gary, "Do you like your Penguin biscuit?"

Chee continued eating, watching curiously as Gary held the wrapper before him. He opened it fully and pointed to the picture.

"That's a penguin Sonny, have you ever seen one?"

Chee was finished eating; he took the wrapper from the boy and looked closely at it.

Terry had his arms out and imitated how a penguin may walk. He shuffled across the grass and started making ducky, quacking noises to Sonny, who looked in fascination between the wrapper and the birdlike boy.

Gary pointed from the picture to Terry.

"That's the penguin Sonny, can you see it?"

Chee's mouth became rounded in thought, almost as if he was trying to understand the comparisons between Terry's imitation, and the picture of the bird thing he held in his hand.

He gave three chirps, looking between Terry who still imitated a noisy penguin making ducky noises, and the picture that intrigued him so.

The little macaque's hands were held out a bit to his side, and then he rocked sideways.

"Terry, look at him!"....

Terry turned to see Sonny imitate him, imitating the penguin, he beamed enthusiastically to Gary

"Come on Gary, follow me".

Then the three waddled in turn around the glade, the boys whooping and hollering in ecstasy, the monkey trying his best to join in with the imitation of the mysterious bird-thing

"Maybe he's seen one in a zoo" giggled Terry, looking behind himself at the monkeys theatrics "he looks as though he knows what we're doin"

"How would he get into a zoo, numpty!?" jibed his little pal, still clucking crazily behind his mate.

Terry looked at him as though he was the stupidest person alive.

"Well he had to escape from somewhere, didn't he, might as well have been a zoo as anywhere else!"

Gary thought about it for a few moments, and then it seemed to make perfect sense.

"Yeah" said the world's smallest cynic "maybe your right enough"

Then he remembered something.

Something quite important.

"Hey wait Terry,"

He rushed over to where his bag lay.

"I forgot this!" He delved excitedly into his bag and stood away from Terry and the monkey.

He stood fifteen yards off them holding it behind his back.

Then he pulled a disposable camera up to his face and shouted to the pair of them.

"Right you two, give me big monkey smiles!"

Terry looked down to his monkey companion, who looked from Gary up to him.

"Do you know how to smile Sonny?"

Then he grinned the widest, gawkiest smile imaginable, trying to show the monkey what he was to do.

"You see?"

The monkey looked up to him, then with a little confusion, over to the other boy.

He was smiling almost as inanely as Terry.

So he lifted his top lip and a second later the camera clicked and a flash lit the glade.

"Brilliant, you take one of me now!"

Terry felt slightly jealous walking away from his little charge; he wasn't too fond of the idea of taking a picture of his monkey and Gary.

He looked down to the camera as he plodded away.

"How do you work this thing?"

"Dead simple, it's all set for the distance, just make sure you stand on the spot where I stood", he pointed to it, "and once you see us through the viewfinder click the black button on the right hand side"

Gary was ready to smile but the camera clicked and flashed as Terry was raising it.

"Ahh, No!!, Terry, there's only two left, make sure you get it right this time, then I can take a surprise one with the last"

He held the camera carefully to his eye.

"'What's the surprise?"

"If I tell you it'll not be a surpr-"

The camera clicked as he shouted across.

"Ach, Terry!"

Terry smiled to himself.

"Sorry..."

Gary shook his head as Terry approached, holding out the camera, smiling as though he was quite pleased with himself.

"Right, take the surprise one!"

Gary swiped the camera from him and mumbled ungraciously as he walked away. He settled on a carefully chosen spot, which was about ten feet away, then nestled the camera onto a tight little nook in a nearby tree.

"Right, don't you move, d'you hear me", he peered through the viewfinder, adjusting the lens as he shouted, "this timer takes ten seconds to click, so when I press, I'll come running and don't let the wee man get frightened" then he looked over the camera.

"D'you think you could do that?"

"Yip"

"Right, on the count of ten" he clicked it then started running.

"Nine! Eight! Seven!"

Chee tensed slightly when he seen the boy run for them.

"Six! Five! Four!"

He jumped up onto Terry's arms watching as both boys chanted the descending numbers.

"Three!Two!One!"

Then Gary rushed by their side and the two boys shouted gleefully toward the camera.

"CHEEEEESE!!!"

They finished the breakfast feast that Terry had spent ages silently preparing as his mother slept upstairs, completely unaware.

It didn't work out too much as was planned, the humans had eaten the monkey's food and with the exception of a mouthful of sandwich and a penguin biscuit bar, Sonny had eaten all the human food. But still, no one complained too much, especially the macaque.

The three mates had played and danced in the sunlit glade all morning and eventually time caught up with them. Both boys had been awake since dawn almost, so it was no surprise that the three were stretched out on a bank beside the small river. Chee rested on Terry's lap, Terry and Gary both lay flat out in the warm sunshine with their heads rested back on their backpacks, and eventually, all three fell into a restful, early morning nap.

Terry felt a nudge sometime after, but continued to sleep...

Just a little nudge, a little monkey sized nudge.

He smiled and fell further asleep.

Casual thoughts and random memories...maybe we'll never go to school again.

His eye's shot open after what seemed like a whole days sleep!!

He immediately sat up and checked his watch, shouting

to awaken his sleeping mate.

"Gary, that's twenty past two!"

Little Gary sat up slowly, rubbing his still sleeping eyes as he came to.

"What time did you say?" he looked over toward his mate, who was staring incomprehensibly around himself, him too half-asleep.

"Sonny's away Gary"...

Terry spoke matter of factly, almost as if he always knew it was going to happen.

He held up the lead and bungee chord, and spoke to it, nodding his head while he spoke, and although he was speaking through dampening eyes, he smiled softly.

"He's off to pastures new" then he looked sadly around the forest as he finished.

"Aren't you son"...

Chapter 27

Armageddon.

13th November.

The little macaque's life was complicated hopelessly on this date, things were happening forty miles north, that would change his life beyond belief, and tragically end the life of his other family members of the colony of macaques back at the Safari Park.

Simian herpes b. virus.

Apparently, completely harmless to Rhesus Macaque's.

But potentially, fatal to humans.

On a deadly par with the lethal flesh-eating Ebola virus, the bug was diagnosed after a series of mandatory health checks on the animals, it was identified in the family of macaques and sadly, the colony was closed down and isolated, within minutes of the terrible news.

Regretfully, there was only one avenue open.

Mass cull.

The three clans seemed to detect intuitively that there was something wrong, roll-houses stopped entering their enclosure, no food was left for them, and they were inspected by dark-uniformed strangers, and for the first time since they could remember, not Har-ree.

But there was one further and potentially devastating complication yet to be discovered.

They checked their records painstakingly, then they checked them again, but incredibly, they couldn't get the numbers to add up.

Incredibly, there was a one year-old male unaccounted for!

The parks authorities, and consequently, Government bodies, were horrified at the news.

An intensive inch-by-inch ground search of the grounds and surrounding area was ordered immediately. It was quickly carried out, but during the massive search of the many huts, cages, lairs and dens, no Rhesus bones or skeletal remains were discovered.

There was no trace of the animal; somehow, amazingly, it had managed to escape the park!

Only then was it learned that a Macaque had been discovered and nearly captured; fortunately the officer it had bitten was wearing gloves and the bite hadn't pierced her skin.

Happily, she was clear.

It was decided at this point not to make the information public.

Due to the mass outcry that was expected over public health, it was deduced that from the date of the sighting, until the dreadful discovery that one of the beasts were missing, there were three clear months.

In the words of one of the Senior Ministers "It was a good, calculated gamble that it was either clear of the virus or dead"

Then he added ominously.

"Or it will be soon"...

Chapter 28

The Deep-Save Incident.

Chee lived and rummaged around the large forest for the next two months, through September and the end of October. He remained in an area roughly five miles square and totally enclosed by the forestation. This was more like the ancient monkey home of his Mothers great fable, but he began to find himself liable to longer and nagging bouts of homesickness. Rhesus monkeys naturally live in troops, even in captivity, the nearest he had found to that kind of feeling since he left the Park was his time spent with the two human boys that had helped and befriended him for those few, funny days after he had been shot with the poisoned, flashing feathers, but now he began to miss his own kind.

He found himself thinking more about his Mother and brother, the other Chee monkeys and now even more than before also, the female monkeys of his age.

Living off the land and scavenging whatever he could come across, his fur thickened in time, and his skin grew taught and rough as the nights started to grow longer. He slowly discovered his frugal existence getting leaner as the days became shorter and colder.

The berries and nuts that he had been feeding upon, which seemed in plentiful supply at one point, were also collected, eaten and stored by the forests many other wild inhabitants. There were squirrels vying with the monkey for the diminishing food supply in and around the trees and many types of birds scouring the upper reaches of the thick foliage and the surrounding shrubbery. For the first time he found himself eating leaves and scrapings of bark, pulled from the branches around him, foxes and badgers also roamed the woods, taking whatever they could find, and like the foxes, the now year-old monkey eventually found himself wandering to the peripheries of the forest and living closer to the extremities, eking out whatever he could in the areas lived in and frequented by the humans.

It seemed to have been raining for days; he sat watching them pass from high above on the outskirts of the town, where the forest thinned to meet it. They were shaded from the cold and incessant rain by coats slung warmly around them, shoes protecting their soft feet from the biting cold, and hats...which at that point, he desperately longed for.

And the rain stoppers, the wonderful looking umbrella's, he watched them, how he would love one, to hold over his head, and keep this rain madness from him.

At best it ran down and onto him in small rivulets, the dots of freezing rain stabbing into his skin and almost making him flinch with each cold maddening spot of it.

At worst it seemed to flow from the great branches above him in streams, just when he thought he might have found the best-protected spot on the tree.

He shivered in the interminable wet coldness; he looked and spied three black birds, which sat just across from him in the branches of another tree.

They seemed content, how could they? How could they become used to this?!

The birds just sat staring into it, somehow switched off to the dementedness that enshrouded him, even more, the constantly lapping rain that continued to pour down around him.

He was almost lunatic with it, the constant, incessant rain, touching him, piercing his skin with each drop.

Much later that night he decided that he had to move and explore the built-up area to protect his sanity against this weather, and to hunt for food; ultimately hunger was now the deciding and overriding factor. He carefully explored through the deserted and poorly lit sections of buildings and soon came to a courtyard which seemed littered with empty boxes, paper and plastic wrapping. He spied a door and noticed it lay ajar, with only a little light in the distance of it. He approached the entrance guardedly, and stood beside it, waiting for any movement which would make him bolt back to the unknown.

Nothing.

No movement, only a little noise, a light humming in the distance.

He put his head in the doorway.

He was stunned immediately, his eye's widened as he tried to take in all that lay around him.

This was a cavernous, and to the monkey's mind, gigantic area, dimly lit, that was literally filled to brim with packages.

It looked to him like food, although the smell to him was new and indescribable. He crept silently to the nearest corner that looked quiet to him, but in truth the night shift had already started and the air was filled with the unknown and continuous noise of forklift trucks, whirring, lifting and laying. Distant shouts and conversations from the store men and shelf stackers echoed through the still air while he sat and took stock of his surroundings. Fluorescent lights hung high in the upper reaches of the store, but their dim and flickering tubes hardly lit the dark and dusty flooring around him.

He froze into a small ball as a sound came closer, the humming became a drone, louder and now more apparent, quickly and silently he pulled himself further into his hidden spot.

He watched from behind a dusty, unused table into the darkest reaches of the store and waited as the noise grew closer. He looked on, hardly daring to breath, at the unknown machine that stopped only ten feet from him. A man sat inside it that made him relax slightly.

He gasped in awe as it extended his arms and stretched high above itself, then lifted a great box from the top shelf, and easily lowered it down.

The man sung to himself as the machine whirred and clanked busily. The little monkey viewed before himself in absolute awe at the wonders ahead and around him.

The yellow machine turned, then whirred away moments after, still with the man humming the tuneless air.

He sat in quiet thought for some moments after that, watching to see if the long armed machine would return, but for the next five minutes or so, it clanked away in the distance.

He rose to investigate in the dull quietness. He stood and slowly put his head around the corner, then viewed the long corridor that the machine had trundled along.

Empty, only long, stacked shelving, all with boxes and shiny packages piled for as high as he could make out.

With his lips rounded in thought, the monkey moved quickly to the shelving.

He looked through the plastic film coating them and tried to look at the labels on the metal tins.

Green peas.

Hundreds of cans.

Next to that was sweet corn, also hundreds of cans of that.

The monkey pushed hard into the clear plastic and his finger emerged on the other side. He waggled his finger through to rub against the label on the can.

Baked beans, he'd never tasted them before, but that didn't stop him from wanting to.

He licked the saliva that was starting to appear on his lips.

Chee walked along the great lines of crates, pallets and boxes of food.

Touching and feeling.

Sniffing and licking.

It was now beginning to dawn on the monkey that he may have landed in food paradise; he was now absolutely surrounded by all kinds of foodstuffs, almost as if he had just dreamt of this moment!

He looked across and above himself and just a few yards along he could see a trolley with loose packages lying opened. This was yoghurts, cheeses and other dairy produce just past its shelf life and prepared for return.

He tore the packages opened and ate as much yoghurt and cheese as a monkey could.

Then walked further into the great store.

He turned a corner and watched someone walk through clear plastic curtains, into an area that seemed better lit, and maybe a little warmer, now he had stopped shivering with the cold but hadn't really warmed through yet.

Again he watched as he approached, bolting from one

hidden spot to another, then he stood at the curtains, looking through them.

Some quiet moments passed, he slipped through the curtains, and again hid as soon as he entered the shiny-floored area.

If the monkey had thought that what was around him was quite wonderful beforehand, then his eyes almost sprung and shot from their sockets at what he beheld when he crept through the clear plastic curtains.

He found himself in the middle of an immense, but almost deserted supermarket, with only a few shelf-stackers mundanely filling, lifting and laying in the distance. Again his mouth rounded in contemplation, he ran quickly to the shelving and could see food, food and more food!

Food Heaven!

It lay all around him; in every direction that he put his head there were great banks of it.

Co-incidentally, he had entered the supermarket at the fresh fruit and veg. department and soon found himself gathering armfuls of fruit and galloping through in the faint night-lights glow, to the darkest and quietest section of the dimmed and almost deserted superstore.

The quietness of the clothing section drew him straight to it, he jumped and landed on a selection of sale items in the children's wear section, shirts, pants and sweatshirts with various motifs emblazoned on them.

He heard footsteps and drew himself further down and into the bank of mixed and multi-coloured clothing, covering himself fully as he hid into it.

Through slats in the side of the box, he noticed a uniformed man approach, thirty yards in the distance.

Now with his breathing rate almost halved, he watched

the man walk forward, then he stopped.

The man leaned down and picked up a kiwi-fruit.

Examined it, then looked around himself.

Then slower forward, he stopped after another ten paces, just short of the clothes bank.

Two grapes, dropped from a bunch....

The man bent and picked them up, with eyebrows lowered suspiciously.

He had no idea he was literally only inches from the monkey, now almost completely holding his breath, and hiding himself and the armful of fruit which had almost given him away.

The man couldn't smell the monkey, but the reek of the human almost petrified the simian, making every hair on the young macaques body stand literally on edge, as he lay in the self-imposed darkness of the box of mixed garments.

It was only through sheer good-fortune and monkey luck, that the man walked on and away, and never noticed a tail sitting upon the sweatshirts and joggers.

A live, macaque tail!

Then, when the security guard was away and out of danger, the tail moved, and again sprang to life.

There was fruit to be eaten!

How good these banana's tasted to him, beautiful little clementine's that drenched his taste buds with delicious, thirst quenching juice. Firm, delicious peaches, then crisp and succulent apples.

He ate so much his stomach ached in pleasure...

Satisfied, with hunger now completely sated, he was full, warm and dry and had no idea what tomorrow might throw his way, all he did know was that tonight had a very nice ending, these were his last, conscious thoughts as his mind drifted aimlessly while he tumbled in the knoll of mixed clothes that was to be his bed for the night, his last, knowing thought,

This hut is good....food is very good...comfortable...warm and dry.

And no cold rains.......

In this place of home....

Chee came to with a crashing, banging and clashing of metal trolleys.

He tried to open his eyes, but the severe light almost blinded him, he had to take time to slowly remind himself of his location, but in truth he had eaten so much and slept so fully, this place now seemed so completely different to the quietness and stillness of the area that he had inhabited last night.

Still under a loose pile of clothing, he screwed his eyes and could slowly make out a tumult of humans walking in and around the area that he had been sleeping in, each one pushing a metal cage thing in front of them. He remained still and unmoving, hoping at some point to rise and escape quietly back through the clear doors then to the safety of the forest covering. Some had children walking by their sides, some were alone, while others walked in pairs, but each seemed intent on what was around them. He remembered the doors that he had entered were just down and across; when things quietened he would bolt the short distance.

How wonderful the forest seemed to him now, rain or not, how safe he would be, up there in the tree's silence, where the peace was broken only by a bird's calling or busy, hungry squirrels rummaging through the canopy.

He saw movement very near, a small, young female walked in his direction.

Chee forced himself lower and deeper into the embankment of garments, hoping the child would pass.

The container swung and swayed with the child's body.

She sung gently to herself as she looked and played with the character clothing, laughing softly whenever she came across anything familiar or funny.

Then he felt the movement stop.

He felt his back bare of clothes, exposed, but still unaware of above himself, with his head still buried in the bowels of it.

"Hello!"

The macaque felt a light tap on his back.

He stayed in exactly the same position.

Then he felt a rub on his neck, which was now exposed.

"Hello boy!"

The light, child voice again, trying to communicate with him, surely this couldn't be dangerous?

He turned around and saw her looking at him, from a foot or so up.

"Hello boy!" she gurgled, "My name's Rebecca, what's yours?"

Incredibly, the monkey answered the question, but in his own Scots Rhesus language.

Just a little succession of six chirps and a short, friendly display of his upper teeth.

"I'm a Chee monkey and I respect your area".....

The child continued to stroke the monkey as he pulled himself further down, always aware that grown humans wandered only feet by at times and in his vulnerable position, he wanted the least amount of his body showing as possible. Chee was thankful when the child tripped off, shouted to someone in the distance, then just dawdled away.

Immersed in the soft, warm darkness that was the cloths pile, he felt he could now quite easily be in the safest spot possible; this hidden den seemed as if it might do for a while yet.

He was so relaxed by this time; he started to think about his next meal.

And immediately salivated.

Quiet gingerly, he erected his head from the mass of clothes and looked hopefully, and a little greedily, toward the fruit display.

The moment his eye's cleared the heap he noticed the kid walking back toward him, only this time she was pulling an adult females hand and leading her to the spot where he lay.

He pulled himself down to the other side of the container, hoping to fool the child....

"Come on Rebecca, you know we have to get your Grannies messages before I go to work!"

The child let go her mother's hand and quickly threw herself up and hung over the container at her waist height then started to rummage through the brightly coloured assortment.

"Where are you Squeaky?" she pulled and pushed the garments as her Mother watched helplessly on. She looked irritably to her watch as the child sang and searched at the same time.

"C'mon Becky!"...she whispered; now beginning to look toward the butchers section.

Was it chicken, or lamb she wanted?

Biting her lip, she started to walk toward the deli.

Better get some coleslaw too!...

"There you are!" she jumped from the container "Mummy he's here, Squeaky's here!"

Little Becky grabbed her Mother's hand and forcibly tried to pull her back.

"This is his house, this is where he stays!"

She found herself looking at a pile, an absolute mishmash of multi-coloured clothing, in no single order whatsoever.

She looked to her daughter, and thought lamb!

"C'mon sweetheart, lets-"

Becky stood with the widest grin that had ever been in her twelve-toothed head.

Pointing.

Then something slowly moved in the clothes-basket...

And at once, as if in a three-dimensional puzzle, a body suddenly became clear to her, a vision which at first she couldn't see, now moved and appeared in her sight!

A monkey!

A live, brown monkey!!

She gaped incredibly downwards and slowly took her daughters hand, still looking at the beast; she could now see apple cores and orange peel!

And banana skins....

She felt ready to erupt, to roar...

She lifted Becky, and ran toward the checkout.

"Do you know you have a monkey in the store?!"

She was pointing frantically toward the clothes section.

People were milling around the area and it was quite clear to him, this was either a leg-pull, or someone was being totally irrational.

"Is there now?"

She held a struggling four-year old in her arms and tried to speak over the child's moans.

And she did speak and act quite irrationally.

"Yes, it's in that remnants box!" she whispered, pointing hurriedly to it.

"The Remnant Box!" he repeated, smiling.

She realised that the duty manager didn't quite take her seriously, who would, so she pulled his lapel and him, further in.

She looked to his lapel badge.

"Listen Mister Thompson, there's a wild ape or monkey, loose and fully grown by the look, and it's hiding in that box over there.

He went to give a slightly foolish reply, and then stopped himself.

It flashed immediately to his mind, crazily he thought.

Of course.

Licking his lips in consideration, he recalled the reports of scavenging from last night, from the night-shift foreman.

Yoghurts, cheeses, milk and some fruit...

The astonishing news report from a few months ago surfaced in his mind.

The Rhesus monkey that was almost captured in Bearsden! He remembered that it had bitten a W.P.C.!

Now, it might make perfect sense!

He stepped a few paces over toward the remnants box, then saw movement in it!

Definite movement!

Brown, animal fur!

A TAIL?

He looked straight over to a uniformed teenage lad who strolled past pushing a trolley loaded with cans. He tried to speak as lowly as possible.

"Tony, get Michael, Andy and Simon and bring them here as quickly as possible!"

The boy went to speak; he was just going for his tea!

The duty manager, Mr Thompson, growled fiercely in his direction.

"Tony, Now!!!"

He turned and smiled back to Rebecca's Mum as pleasantly as possible.

And lifted an eyebrow.

"How big is it?"

She looked toward it, and thought fleetingly.

"Just a bit smaller than her" she nudged the child up in her arms as she spoke astonishingly of her, "She was playing with it, clapping and rubbing it!"

Rebecca giggled at the thought, then struggled to get put down and back to it, her new friend.

He placed his fingers on his lips thoughtfully.

"Did it let her?"

She nodded quickly, "Yes, it seemed to be friendly enough, but you know"...

"You never know!" he finished off for her, shaking his head a little fearfully.

They both looked over when they saw another movement in the garment box, Rebecca squealed with delight from the twenty yards off. He looked over the packed aisles rubbing his chin grimly then shouted a twenty-something girl over.

"Sarah, c'mere!"

She came and stood beside the two other adults and Rebecca.

"Sarah, I want you to go to the office and phone the police"

Her eyes opened wide as she listened along.

Then she found herself looking in the same direction as the other three, to the still deserted box of remnants.

Again, the contents shifted a little!

"Tell them that I think we have the escaped monkey from Bearsden!"..., Sarah breathed in sharply while Rebecca giggled ridiculously, speaking and laughing aloud now, to her new friend, Squeaky.

The Duty Manager stepped forward to intercept a shopper who neared the garments box.

"Excuse me Ma-am!"

The elderly lady stopped and looked over.

"Please don't enter that area Ma-am, it's just been washed and the floor's still a bit slippery"

The lady looked to the bone-dry floor, then quite puzzled, replied, "But it doesn't look so"....

He put out a restraining arm from the fifteen yards off, "Please Ma-am, come back from it!"

He organized the emergency procedures superbly, almost expertly.

Staff had started to clear the many shoppers, gently explaining that there was a fire drill to perform every six months, and this was now the time for it. The back area, the clothing section, was cordoned off and friendly staff stood by, warding any stragglers off and out of the store. The Police had been informed and were on their way, all in all the Duty Manager, Mr.Thompson, had every right to be pleased with his performance.

He was quite sure that his bosses down in Harlow, would be as pleased with the evacuation as he was.

Maybe even pleased enough to give him a bonus, or a rise!

What about promotion?

His chest swelled as he reflected.

What he didn't know, and couldn't realise, was that he had done his job too well.

For as the store was emptied, the monkey decided that now was the time to try the escape, and in one of the few occasions that the Duty Managers eye's strayed from the clothes box, the monkey slipped from it!

Scurrying along the last aisle of clothing, he stopped when he saw a lad guarding the aisle and pulled into a line of coats, in hangers on a metal rail.

Just as he did that, three uniformed policemen were brought into the building and shown the box where the monkey supposedly lay.

Mr. Thompson was asked to stay well back and Rebecca and her Mother waited in his office, with a cup of tea and some juice.

Watching across the aisles in multi-screens.

The three policemen slowly neared the box, now with nets and wearing thick gloves, hopefully they could have it snared before the R.S.P.C.A. would have been called.

Three ran to it, and covered the box with the net, then the transportation cage was brought out and they waited for the monkey to show face.

They should have realised that this was just too easy, they put prods down into the bank of clothing, Mr Thompson watched keenly on, Rebecca and her Mum, peered out from the office.

Nothing.

They put more prods in, softly jabbing into the clothing, but nothing moved in the pile.

Nothing.

The Policemen looked over to Mr Thompson, the Duty Manager.

He looked up and across the aisles to his office, and Rebecca's Mum.

She, in bewilderment, stared down to Rebecca.

Where?

Soon they were gathered and standing over the pile, with the policemen listening and watching as Mr.Thompson and Rebecca's Mum tried to explain.

There were definitely apple cores and orange skins...

But it didn't seem to make sense.

Mr Thompson hadn't actually seen it.

Rebecca's Mum swore she thought she saw it, but now didn't seem quite sure.

Rebecca?

She was only four and a half...

They were just about to open the doors to the public, Wendy Taylor stood by with the key to open the electric slide doors and let the police out.

The lad, the last lad on the last aisle, had just started to return to the checkouts.

When something whizzed by the last aisle.

He ran to the end to follow the browny-red blur.

"MR THOMPSON!"

He got to the aisle ends and then couldn't believe what he was watching

A brown monkey was pulling at the locked, store doors, struggling and heaving at them to gain its freedom!

Then it turned and saw him, watching it!!

Simon roared for all that he was worth!

"MISTER THOMPSON, THERE'S A MONKEY TRYING TO GET OUT INTO THE BACK STORES!!!!"

He watched on as the beast leapt away from the locked doors, and then ran down the next aisle of biscuits, crackers and cookies. He followed, shouting to alert his boss and the Police.

"He's on row thirteen, at the biscuits!"

The monkey reached the end of the aisle, but spied the assortment of humans alerted, and now ready to pursue him.

He climbed the seven-foot high shelf, spilling packets and packages as he scaled it, and from the top of the shelf, leapt spectacularly to the other side, sending bottles and containers crashing and spinning to the floor where he landed.

Then he took off again, now with the Police and Duty Manager following his noisy and extremely messy progress from aisle to aisle, walking along the end of the aisles, from one end of the superstore to the other, thirty metres from the beast.

Over one hundred shoppers now stood and watched the unbelievable events unfold through the clear line of windows, which ran the length of the store. As the monkey ran and leapt from line to line of shelving, they followed his progress, cheering each time he leapt and landed, each shopper vying with the others for a better view of the now incredible incident!

Chee stood at the last shelf and watched around himself in the near deserted supermarket.

Now it had been cleared of all but only a few of the staff, leaving only the Duty Manager, a young girl who stood beside the locked sliding doors with a key to open and close them, and the three uniformed Policemen.

He was well aware of them; he remembered the collection of them that tried to capture him all those days ago when he first escaped into the forest that was his home then. He watched them as they spoke and watched him, pointing in his direction, and planning his next route from where he sat and eyed them.

His deep brown eyes moved constantly from point to point, every few seconds almost.

Every eye movement was a separate thought, every time he turned his head to look, he viewed it a different way, another route to escape from them.

From his vantage point at the back of the store, on top of the second last row of shelving, he had perfect knowledge of them and their whereabouts.

He saw them nod, point, and then approach different positions.

Each one of the officers stood in rows before him and started to approach the middle of each aisle, and when they came close enough he could see they held poles with nets attached. He ran quickly from the rear and soon scrambled over the rows of shelving to the other side of the hall.

By this time there were boxes, bottles, tins and many other packages strewn across the aisles, disturbed and spilled open by the monkey in his hurry to escape the humans. The Policemen regrouped and it was decided that they would approach it a little differently this time.

The last Officer, the furthest away, would enter the

aisle three rows from the monkey and stand in the centre, three rows down. As he did this, the second would enter the second aisle and walk to the centre, two rows from the watching monkey. Chee nibbled the edges of his fingernails as he watched them try to cut off his escape route. He waited as the last officer walked slowly to put himself in place.

He could now see it.

One in place in the fourth aisle, one in the third and now the last one walking slowly toward him in the second. He smiled up to the monkey from fifteen yards off, holding the net behind his back as he attempted to entice it down.

He didn't fool the now street-wise macaque for a second, swaying a banana up toward it.

He simply dropped down to the other side, the blind side of the shelving, and waited the next development. The Officer shouted to the Store Manager who watched from the end of the aisle.

"HE'S ON THE BACKSIDE, THE OTHER SIDE OF THE VERY LAST ROW!" he pointed over the shelving. "WILL YOU WALK DOWN THE AISLE AND MAYBE HE'LL TRY TO RUN FOR IT!"

The crowd watched as Mr.Thompson nodded, then walked slowly to the end of the aisle, the very last row.

The monkey spied the man the moment he turned into the aisle, but he sped off in the opposite direction, attempting to outrun his pursuers.

"HE'S RUNNING TOWARD THE FAR END OF THE AISLE!"

Thompson could only watch as the beast sped down the row of shelving, then turned to disappear from his sight at the end of it. The first Policeman had no chance of catching him, but the second and third were quickly placing themselves in position as the frantic beast was bolting down the end corridor. The second could only throw his net at the monkey, but it bounced off and harmlessly away from him, then the third found himself in position at the same time as the monkey appeared on the scene!

For a few seconds man and macaque stared at each other, the second officer watched wide-eyed behind them as he struggled to erect himself with the first.

Mr.Thompson now watched helplessly from behind.

The monkey stopped in his tracks three metres' in front of the Policeman.

The Officer stood with his arm outstretched and swaying the net perilously close to the beast's head.

The man smiled, and then spoke gently to it...

"C'mon pal, who's a good boy then?"

By this time the monkey's eyes were flashing in every direction in front and behind himself, the two other Officers and the Duty Manager had now gathered only a few tense metres away, and were now ready to encircle him.

The crowd on the outside was growing by the moment and watched on keenly as the monkey decided on the next course of events. The viewing audience swayed as one almost, as they watched him firstly jerk himself around, then leap in the direction of the high shelving again, nets flashed around him, the Policemen tried firstly to catch him with their swooping nets, then flapped the sticks uselessly, trying to hit him with them and knock him from the six foot high run, but he soon passed them, and in one amazing leap, he landed on another rack, over two metres away!

Then he crossed the aisle and slowly climbed the fourth rack of shelving.

After that there was nothing to hold him back and soon he was back at the other end, watching the humans re-group and catch their breath after the brief period of hectic activity.

By this time Chee was also heaving for breath, leaping and climbing the few hundred yards of shelving was beginning to take its toll on the simian and his lungs pulled air in heavily during the time he took to recover.

But things were now about to get worse for him; a ringing, metallic tapping on the glass sliding doors broke the uneasy silence.

The girl on the door watched as a team of R.S.P.C.A. Inspectors waited for entry.

Instinctively Chee lowered his head and swallowed solemnly, he remembered them also from his first time around.....

Three men and two women, now the force against him amounted to nine; he held his fingers and counted unconsciously to himself.

One hand wrapped around four fingers.

He noticed that the plastic curtains he had arrived through last night were covered by metallic, sliding doors, now pulled over and locked.

As were all the other doors in the facility, he had no idea how he would escape this scene, again his eyes flashed around the store and his mind worked on his next route.

There were now masses of people at the windows, each jostling with others, goggle-eyed almost, and more rushed to join them from other shops and outlets as word spread of the incident no one could quite believe, an escaped monkey in the giant Deep-Save Hypermarket, now being hunted by a mixed force of Police and R.S.P.C.A. Inspectors!

He saw light blue suited men walk toward him and leapt down from the top of the shelving. He ran to the right hand side of the store, the far off side from the watching public, who now cheered him wildly on. He could hear the hunters scarper after him; the store rang out with hollow shouts, thudded footsteps, orders and collaborations of the pursuing humans, all in order to capture the monkey!

Some Officers saw a flash of fur whiz by the top end of the third aisle.

"IT'S APPROACHING THE END OF THE FOURTH!"

They gathered quickly, at the end of the fourth, fifth and sixth rows, each now with a net and ready to pounce whenever it came into view.

Then they were at the end of the fourth, it could have come no further...

The two Inspectors who ran toward the end of the line of shelving looked beyond it, in the direction of the other two in the third row.

"CLEAR HERE!"

"AND HERE!" responded the other, they stood back and carefully inspected the area around themselves where the beast was spied only moments earlier.

"It's here somewhere, it must be!"

The Policemen looked toward each other, then slightly nervously to the R.S.P.C.A. Inspector.

The loaded dart gun, pointed in the direction they thought the beast lay.

"Make sure you keep that thing pointed away from us, will you?"

He quite guiltily pulled it downward, out of harm's way.

The gathered force then started the thorough examination of the area, the few square metres they had last seen it disappear into. Foodstuffs and household goods were lying disturbed all around the store by this time and the mixed assembly carefully pulled dozens of packs and boxes from shelves, piles of tins and jars were sent crashing down, strewn across the floor in the spot that the beast had last been seen.

No one could believe it, the macaque just seemed to have vanished into thin air!

They began to look and search beyond the immediate area after some time, there really were so many places it could now be lurking, but they were sure they would discover it soon.

Everyone was sure it was hidden in this, the far-off section of the superstore. The floor was now cluttered with packs of soap powder, cleansing fluids, plastic containers of bleach, toilet and kitchen cleaners, mops, bin bags and pot-scourers, all lying on the floor and cleared from the immediate vicinity of the monkeys last sighting. It was then agreed to start to work their way back, they must have missed it.

Soon they were clearing the shelves of anything large enough to hide the beast and were working their way methodically out of the far corner of the store.

Then a piercing cry rang out, followed by a muffling

and crashing noise!

The girl on door duty, on the exact opposite side of the hall from the activity, watched the movements, only fifty meters away from her, then turned and cried out to her Manager.

"IT'S COMING OUT ON THIS SIDE MISTER THOMPSON!!!"

She covered her mouth as she pointed to the spot!

"IT'S HERE!!!

The macaque emerged from the other end of the third row of supermarket shelving, and at the exact opposite side from the searching posse of Police and R.S.P.C.A. Inspectors.

He had slowly and painstakingly crawled and scrambled his way along the inside of the shelving, along the dark and dusted flooring, to the other side of the hall that he had entered!

A presentation of kitchenware came crashing unceremoniously down around him, as he unearthed himself, dusted, dirtied and clinging in spider webs, from the bowels of the shelving!

Immediately the hunting party turned and ran in stunned groups, leaping over the spilled packages and tins in their rush to capture the bewildered simian. As the monkey ran along the corridor, he could see groups of them get nearer to him with every aisle he passed, he was haring as fast as he possibly could, and as he ran the full length of the corridor he could also see the gathered crowd through the windows only feet from him, as he ran along the end corridor, they ran alongside him, following every movement that was made inside the superstore!

The humans were now only twenty yards behind him

and he could see the end of the corridor looming ahead. He was at most only fifteen feet from the girl on the door and the chasing pack only moments from encircling and his inevitable capture!

Then unbelievably, a door rumbled open as he passed it; he froze almost, then turned to see it slide open!

After the half second that it took to view it, he turned and saw the approaching force, and almost to a man, they shouted to the horrified door operative.

"CLOSE THE DOOR!!!!"

She had forgotten to turn the locking mechanism after the R.S.P.C.A. had entered the building last!

The Manager, Mr.Thompson, quickly put his hand up and indicated that she should turn the key into the closed and locked position.

The Policemen, as frozen in position as the monkey and the R.S.P.C.A Inspectors and the hundreds watching outside, also urged her, all with their arms pointing to the offending ring of keys, still on the automatic mode.

"LOCK THE DOOR WENDY!!!"

She looked to it, staring at it, and they all shouted louder...

"LOCK THE DOOR WENDY!!!"

The stupefied operative tried to make up for her mistake and stretched over to flick the keys into the closed mode. The doors hummed and started to draw to a close, but just as they did so, the macaque bolted forward and peeled himself through them, the air around him suddenly thick with nets and poles thrown at him by his pursuers.

And just as the doors pulled shut, a coloured arrow fell to the floor, clinking harmlessly off the metal frame of the door.

The monkey looked down quickly, and remembered.

He ran forward, then another door slid open, he looked behind himself and saw the gang of chasing humans wait at the closed door and remonstrate with the girl, now it remained impassibly locked and blocking their exit!

The macaque scrambled through the second door and then found himself thrust amongst a shrieking, gasping crowd of almost two hundred humans, with only a few Police men and woman trying to keep them in some kind of order for their own safety, in the enclosed shopping arcade. The monkey had never seen so many people before in his short life, and stood for some seconds, frightened and bewildered at the very sight of them before him. Luckily there was no time for any kind of planning or thought; he turned to see both doors behind him slide effortlessly open.

The Police and R.S.P.C.A. Inspectors emerged from the superstore, bolting forward in complete disarray, but now freed and fully intent on the monkey's capture.

With no time to think, Chee bolted away from the force only yards behind him and delved into the horrified masses!

He ran forward and into them, the stunned crowd's reaction was like a hot knife through a block of butter, they stood back and formed a fearful path, a channel, which the monkey stormed through, not daring to look backward! Shoppers stood and watched unbelievably, dozens filming on their mobiles, some pulled back, bewildered parents held onto excited children, seasoned security guards were absolutely astonished, pensioners gasped onward, but oddly, some people were wide eyed and smiled at the confounding sight, the monkey and the pursuing pack, flashing and crashing across their vision!

Now over a dozen uniformed men and women, complete with hunting nets and cages, barking into radio hand-sets and vainly chasing a rapidly accelerating year-old Rhesus Macaque, followed by half the shoppers in the mall, trailing husbands, wives, children pensioners and banging, clattering shopping trolley's!

The Police tried to stop the crowds of shoppers from following the chase but it was completely in vain, then crazily, the monkey started to run up the down-moving escalators, that cut back his lead somewhat and by the time he had struggled to the top, the posse was almost behind him and at his heels! He continued to gallop along the upper level, to confound a new and equally disbelieving line of shoppers and workers, watching a monkey and endless lines of humans waiting to get off the escalator at his back and chase him along the first floor of the mall!

Ladies went to faint, incredulous men stood protectively over their wives and children and security guards communicated feverishly through portable hand-sets as the beast sped past, but in truth, it was now starting to get away from the many that hunted him, and the complete and utter madness only ceased when the beast scuttled up some scaffolding erected for some light maintenance, and disappeared thankfully into the ducts of the ceiling, and from there, further into the bowels of the multi-blocked shopping mall.

He found himself in the darkened guts of the building; he was safe, surely, at this spot.

He had ran and crawled along in the growing darkness for some time, then he lay quietly, listening for any sound emanating from the darkness that encompassed him.

But now, all seemed quiet, the only sound to break the black silence....

His own breathing, heaving within him.

Three chirps, a hollow moan, and two high vocal-utterances.

Chee's a good monkey, not a bad monkey.....

Chapter 29

Out in the Open.

Terry came back to his home at four thirty on Saturday, just as he was starting to think about his dinner. They had patrolled the Country Park since leaving their houses at nine-twenty that morning, both him and Gary had covered almost every blade of grass, almost wrenching their necks from their sockets, looking up every tree for him.

Sadly, they found no sign of Sonny.

The park had resounded with the boy's shouts and whistle's, some concerned folk thought they had lost a dog.

Eventually it became apparent to both of them that sadly, the little monkey was only passing through their lives.

He tripped upstairs a little dejectedly, but in truth he was already beginning to get over it, his mind was now half on the game of football arranged for Sunday, between them and the guys that stayed in Brediland Road, should be good, he considered...

Sonny had been an unforgettable experience, a brilliant and bedazzling two days in their lives that he was sure they'd remember forever.

He let himself in, kicked off his muddy shoes, and then went to walk upstairs.

"TERRY!"

His Mother...Jeez.....

"What is it?" he just wanted to go up and listen to some music.

"DOWN HERE RIGHT NOW!"

He tutted and turned on the stair, what does she want?

His parents were waiting in the living room for his entry.

Both looked straight-faced and very serious.

And directly at him.

He had no idea there was a problem, it crossed his mind that the monkey might have poo'd somewhere.

He had to struggle from smiling at the idea.

"What?"

She looked indignantly from him, then to his Dad. He watched Terry with what seemed like a look of despondency, disappointment.

She started, her face scowling and glowing red as she addressed him.

"Thought you swapped schoolbags with Gary Adamson?"

She held up the bag that they had carted Sonny about in.

He nodded back without speaking.

She dropped the old bag then lifted his sports bag; the one Gary was supposed to have.

"I thought he", she nodded angrily in the direction of Gary's house, "was supposed to have this bag!"

Terry flustered his answer.

"He did...for a day or two...then he gave me it back"...

His Mother took her steely look from him momentarily to his Dad, and then she opened the bag.

She pulled a car registration plate from it.

Initially the boy was gob-smacked!

She laid it on the table then delved back into the bag.

His Mother struggled to release a wheel trim, leering at her child as she did so, then she brought out a Volkswagen logo and carefully placed it on the table beside the rest of the pile.

"You better have a very good explanation!"....

By now she was irate, red-faced; he could see blood vessels starting to bulge around her neck!

Her eyes were opened the widest he could ever remember, this was the angriest he could ever remember seeing his always-doubtful Mother!

And he just wanted to laugh!

The note that was left explained it all; he could remember it exactly, word for word;

He will exchange gifts with you for food!

He could feel his lips curing up dangerously at the edges.

He could feel the muscles of his cheeks lifting and pulling at his lips to smile!

The laughter that welled inside him was just about to burst and erupt from within him!!

"What have you got to say Terry?"

Aw no Dad, don't ask me anything! Please don't ask me to speak, I'll blow it, I know I will!!!

His face had now become a parody, in holding back the rivers of laughter, which were now about to drown him, his mouth had become twisted and his eyes watered with the well of joy that he struggled so much to hold back!

He knew it could go at any second!!

To his Mum and Dad, their child looked sad and remorseful, a tear of guilt had welled up so much in his eye, it had started to trickle down his face, they exchanged a quick glance with each other, it would be soon...

Young Terry might have made it, if only his Father hadn't spoken to him. If his rather serious and always suspicious Mother had carried on questioning him, he might have made it through.

He winced as his Father went to speak, and repeated the question he asked him earlier.

"What have you got to say son?"

He could feel it leaving him; he now had absolutely no control over it.

"How did these things get into your bag?"

"IT WAS...IT WAS..A-!!"

Both parents looked to the other.

"AAAAAAAAHHHHHHHHHHAAAAAAAAAA!!!!!"

He collapsed into a heap as it left him, and as he did, his Mum and Dad looked appropriately disturbed while their sorry son wailed wretchedly on the floor before them.

Big Terry looked to Sheila and nodded, as if to say, this will be a lesson for him.

Then both of them approached and Dad bent down to turn him.

They turned from the glazed eyes, the near maniacal expression which lurked on the floor underneath them.

They could now see him laughing uncontrollably; he looked up to them and shouted through a torrent of laughter.

"IT WAS A MONKEY!!"

They looked horribly to one another, then back down to him.

"THATS WHAT PUT THEM THERE, IT WAS A MONKEY!!!"

"HHHHAAAAAAAAAAHHHHHHAAAAAAAAHH HHAAAAAAAHHHAA!"

He kept thinking to himself, Gary would love this; he

would be as bad as me!!!

Sheila stormed out of the door and into the hallway, "THATS IT BIG TERRY, I'M DEFINATELY PHONING THEM THIS TIME, HE'S ON SOMETHING!!!"

Now she was convinced.

First it was smoking; nearly a full year ago, God only knows what that Adamson boy had them doing now.

Drugs, the biggest fear in her life, she was terrified that he would get mixed up with them, in a way she always knew they would come knocking on her door one day.

Now this...it looked hopeless, she was definitely going to phone them and get him put away if she had to, if she thought it would keep him away from them.

His Dad looked from him, lying and laughing helplessly on the living room floor, then stood up and followed his wife outside.

He skelped his hopeless son's leg in annoyance as he erected himself.

Through his laughter he heard them storm at each other in the hall.

"CAN YOU IMAGINE THEM TAKING HIM AWAY SHEILA? HE'S ONLY A TEN YEAR-OLD BOY, YOU DON'T KNOW WHAT IT'LL DO TO HIM!"

The phone was lifted as she attempted to dial the Police, then his Dad slammed it back down. Young Terry heard them shout at each other in the hall, the phone had been lifted and slammed down so many times it must have been broken.

"Sheila, think of what you're doing'" he tried to reason for a last time, "He's only a kid!"

She looked over his shoulder, and then suddenly, she was breathing slower, easier.

She replaced the receiver softly on its mount.

Big Terry looked behind himself, and then saw is son standing at the living room door, watching them.

He held the door open and invited them back into the living room, so that he could explain himself.

He smiled warmly, and warned them to be patient with him.

"Cos what I'm about to tell you" he had their favourite impish smile while he spoke.

"Will take some believing!"…

Chapter 30

The CCTV Mechanic.

"What's to report then Tom?"

Tom turned from the banks of television monitors and glided the swivelled chair over the few yards to his nightshift replacement.

"What's to report!?" he repeated unbelievably, his face set in an incredulous grin, "Did you not hear about it?"

He shrugged nonchalantly "Hear about what?"

Tom then swung back to the bank of screens and controls.

"I've been trying to phone you all day!" he giggled lightly as he spoke, "Watch the top right hand set"

"Deep-Save?"

"Yeah, keep watching"

He placed his hat on the rack and rested on his oppo's seat back as the screen flashed to life. They watched the crowds of shoppers congregate at the outside windows, and then move en masse, along its length.

A robbery? He thought.

Then the masses moved quickly along to the other side, helped quickly along by Tom's fast-forward video techniques.

Then Policemen appeared, waited at the locked doors, and gained entry.

"Somebody robbing the place?"

"No, but keep watching Jack, this is amazing stuff!"

The crowd fast-forwarded up and down a few more times, then Tom slowed the pictures to normal as the second force appeared.

"Here's a little clue for you" he turned and his eyes twinkled in his pals direction "That's the R.S.P.C.A. waiting to get in"

Jack nodded thinking he understood, a dog or cat in the store, maybe even a bird?

He smiled as the crowd fast-forwarded down, then back up, he watched younger folk racing ahead, vying for the best view, then his face screwed to watch the finer detail as the video slowed to normal pace.

People crowded the doorway, over one hundred; he could see the excitement rise to something approaching fever-pitch in the silent video footage.

"It's not so clear just yet, but keep watching, you won't believe it"

At that moment the great doors slid back, then the crowd just seemed to open, a yawning passage was somehow created, people panicked, pushing others aside, amazingly others tried to jump up from behind and gaped for a better view.

Then a small dark body appeared through the massive ruck of humans.

It stood in the open and viewed its strange new surroundings for some seconds, and then it bolted forward, ahead of the force of chasing humans, and into the masses of shoppers, still unaware of the drama which had broken around them.

"Is that a monkey?"

Tom nodded, grinning as broadly as a Cheshire cat, "Watch monitor fifteen now for a clearer view!"

This film showed the monkey closer, it was still low definition film, and because of the animal's speed, it was slightly blurred, but still...

Jack watched with growing astonishment as the monkey ran some distance, through two more monitors. It then escaped after climbing the scaffolding and crawling through the open gap in a roof.

So, after a complete breakdown of the day's events and passing on emergency phone numbers, Tom left the security unit and Jack prepared himself for the night ahead.

Flask of tea, four cheese and tomato sandwiches, Tom Clancy's latest novel and tonight's Evening Times, that should see him through his Saturday night twelve-hour shift.

He had a quick glance at the number scribbled on the pad to contact in case the beast showed its face again, but privately, no one expected it to, didn't matter what the guy from the R.S.P.C.A. recommended, it should make its way out of the store and away from East Kilbride soon enough.

"Probably won't see it again" advised Tom as he left the building.

A snippet of the animals blurred escape had appeared on the short Scottish weekend news at six fifteen, it wasn't noticed by any of the Dunbar's or Connolly's, but an old man in Bearsden sat and smiled happily at the scrap of news that had escaped most of the country's lazy weekend attention.

"Yes" Hector nodded to himself "That's my wee Sonny"....

10.25.

Jack stretched back and yawned wearily, maybe go and stretch my legs now, he thought.

He threw an uncompleted crossword annoyingly down,

walked to the rack and pulled on his jacket.

He had felt the screens drawing his eyes all night.

Fifteen dull, unmoving screens, he tried to look away from them now and again, such was the wearying effect these things were having on his eyesight

He rubbed them and turned slowly to go, but wait, cigarettes!

He stretched across the desktop, and picked the pack and lighter and turned to go.

Then a dull shadow seemed to cross the room.

He turned quickly to the screens, but nothing moved, again he rubbed his sore eyes, definitely need to get new specs!

He turned the key in the door and made to exit the white-lighted room, but again.

Again, a shadow...

He looked back to the bank of screens and then, monitor twelve.

It seemed to shake a little, his face fell into a suspicious frown while he walked back in.

Jack's lighter fell loosely to the ground while he watched the screen shake further.

Then an image covered the screen.

Unfocussed, the camera tried to automatically re-adjust on the form which blocked its vision. Its mechanism automatically rolled one way, then the other, but after some moments he could make it out, in almost full glorious Technicolor.

The monkey staring into the camera, at location twelve, just outside Marks and Spencers!

He sat down staring at the screen and marvelled at the staggering sight before him.

Yes, a wild Rhesus, looking directly into the screen, absolutely fantastic!

The thought crossed his mind.

I'd better phone that number...right .now......

777ooooHis hand felt blindly to his right and he padded about for the telephone, he literally couldn't move his eyes from the screen. The beast looked around the camera, its deep brown eyes, immersed in thought, lips rounded and eyebrows again forming the long thoughtful ridge across his brow. He moved his head out, then back into the camera's vision, all the time, the camera clicked and whirred crazily, automatically trying in vain to keep up with the macaque's appearances in and out of its line of vision.

Then Jack's face fell, when the screen became dead......

Chapter 31

Rogue Macaque!

The Minister for Health had decided it was now time to deal personally with the case of the escaped and potentially disease-ridden Macaque. They now knew its almost exact whereabouts' and three separate teams of Public Health Animal Inspectors had been dispatched by the Ministry to locate and neutralise the beast.

The Mall was now closed to the public, Policemen were placed at strategic point's around the units and absolutely no one without personal authority was allowed to come anywhere near the deserted location. Car parks were cordoned off with red and white 'Animal Disease' warning tape and patrolled, armed Policemen waited on every flat rooftop, peering through glinting binoculars. They kept in constant radio contact, the small security office now manned exclusively by members of H.M Forces.

Each monitor was viewed constantly with information being exchanged and updated regularly.

An armed Policeman stood guard while an electrical contractor had been brought in to repair the security camera that the macaque had left dangling from its mounts.

Almost as if it had been trying to dismantle, then steal it!

This was too much to contemplate and it was decided that the securing nuts and bolts must have worked their way loose through the years.

Of course.

Sunday afternoon led slowly to evening, Inspectors and Policemen had trawled through the rooftops, corridors and basements, almost dissecting the guts of the buildings, combed the vast amounts of ducting and heavy piping, but much to everyone's growing dismay, there were no signs of the macaque.

No dens, no trails of food, and no excrement.

A Public Health Message was screened on local television in the Glasgow area that Sunday evening. The situation was now developing into a potential local health disaster scenario, the stills from the security camera that the macaque had discovered, and had tried to dismantle, were now, almost surreally displayed, with an accompanying, chilling warning.

The beast was now identified as the same one that had escaped from the Wildlife Park four months earlier.

No-one could offer any explanation as to how it managed to travel so far from its home, but it was now recognized as part of the diseased troop that had been culled in Stirling, a week earlier.

It was strenuously advised that no member of the public was to approach it; a contact phone number was emblazoned across the bottom of the screen beside the close-up picture of the animal.

No-one was left in any doubt; this animal was extremely dangerous, and no matter how cute it may appear, it should not be confronted on any account!

Monday morning, 8.35.

Terry Connolly and Gary Adamson were on their way to school and along with three other lads, and had entered the local newspaper shop for their daily dose of sweets, juice and crisps.

Terry stood waiting his place in the queue and Gary wandered to the magazine section to sneak a look at the pop-music news.

But as he approached the crowded magazine rack, he couldn't believe his eyes.

He stood back, stepping into a child behind him, as he tried to take it in.

There in front of him, stunning him completely, on every newspapers front page, was a full-blown colour picture of the little monkey that had befriended them those few short months ago!

On every newspapers front page, his face peered industriously into the camera.

"Terry"...

He was surprised that words could leave his lips; he spoke again, unable to take his vision away from the bank of colour pictures.

"Terry, C'mere!".....

Terry turned from his place in the queue and looked for his pal in the crowded shop.

"Where are you?"

He walked closer to where the voice had come from, broke his way through a pile of laughing and giggling bodies, then, just as his friend, words failed him...

They both looked on in the following moments without speaking, both literally incapable of any movement.

"That's Sonny Terry"...

He only nodded along, but his eyes were starting to moisten, they were struggling to take it in, not so much the pictures emblazoned across every spread-sheet and Daily, but the banner-headlines, which accompanied.

FUGITIVE!

WANTED, DEAD OR ALIVE!

And

DANGER, ESC-APE!!!

"What do they mean?"

Gary pulled a newspaper down and began scanning furiously!

"They're saying he's diseased!?"

Tears lined Terry's face as he ran to the check-out. He threw a fifty-pence coin through the ruck of children and adults onto the counter, towards the perplexed assistant, then both boys hurried from the shop.

Chapter 32

Better Record this...

George Dunbar settled comfortably back into his chair. His tea was finished, dishes were washed, put by and Jill was working back shift.

Luckily for her, he thought...

He smiled toward the screen, then turned the volume higher as the credits began to roll, the first and foremost item on the Scottish news?

The small macaque, still loose and evading capture at the shopping mall in East Kilbride, just south of Glasgow.

It still wasn't known if the beast was infected with the Simian Herpes B virus, so the Teams of Government Health Inspectors and the Police remained on a state of high alert, and the mall remained closed. As the program drew on, the female presenter introduced Benjamin Walsh, a longhaired, bearded and bespectacled expert on the breed. He spoke on at length about the breed, mostly boring research material, but as he neared the end of his spot, he worryingly proclaimed that it was possible for the beast to transfer the disease through saliva, as in a case in America, where a child had died from the disease, after a Macaque had spat at her.

Every parent watching held their child closer on hearing the dreadful news.

He then re-iterated that the beast shouldn't be approached, on any account, it was basically wild, and not used at all, to human contact, "no matter how cute, cuddly, or hungry it may seem"

He then gave the case of the Policewoman who was

bitten the few months earlier as an example of how nasty things could turn.

"This could have been a fatality, rather than just the bite it had proved, but that was months ago", he worryingly warned, "Now, who knows?".....

The presenter turned to the camera with a suitably sombre expression.

"We have been contacted by various parties during the past few days and I'd like to introduce a concerned group, who would like to say a few words"; she raised her eyes accordingly, "surprisingly in the monkeys favour"

The camera swept to a party of mixed individuals.

Sheila Connolly sat uncomfortably, wringing her hands in her lap; sitting to her left was her son Terry.

He sat rigidly, staring awkwardly around himself and shyly upward toward the camera.

Then his pal Gary, who as usual, seemed to be taking things in his stride.

Hector Kerr sat back in his seat, seemingly relaxed and prepared for the interview.

Two females sat next, Mother and daughter, Susan and Lorna-Ann Muir.

Lastly, there was the monkey's Keeper at the Safari Park, Harry Ramsey, dressed seemingly for the occasion with brown bib overalls, red check shirt, heavy boots and socks and a ragged cowboy style hat, which he sat on his lap.

But there was a sad and hollow look about him as he crossed his legs, pulling the durable boot high into his lap.

The presenter looked to her hastily prepared notes.

"Mrs. Muir, I think we should start with you, what was you experience with the monkey?"

Susan Muir's eyes dropped to the floor briefly as she thought, then she looked sideways back to the interviewer.

"I guess it made its own way into our house, this was during that hot spell, in August"

The presenter nodded, remembering.

"Our youngest daughter, Tracy, went into the kitchen and poured herself a drink from the fridge"

Again, the presenter listened closely.

Susan glanced over to her other daughter, who nodded slowly.

"Then Lorna went into the kitchen and discovered the animal pulling all sorts from the fridge"

Now the presenter looked horrifically on, but Susan and Lorna were smiling softly.

"When it saw us, it ran upstairs and away from us"

"Did it attempt to bite anyone?"

"No"

"Was it vicious or aggressive?"

She shook her head lightly, "I've got to say at the time, we were all very alarmed, we'd never seen a monkey up close before, never mind finding one in your fridge", she smiled, " but, no, it didn't seem violent or aggressive, just scared, maybe"

Lorna sat nodding in agreement.

The presenter turned to her.

"What were your memories of the occurrence Lorna?"

She shrugged lightly, "I remember being more surprised than anything, I certainly don't remember being scared of it, I don't think any of us were", she looked toward the expert, "At no time did it try to scratch, bite, or spit at anyone, and we probably made things worse by trying to catch it"

He jumped in, just as the child had finished speaking.

"Ah well, you shouldn't have my dear, this is, as I've just said, a wild animal, it's already bitten once, now it may be just a matter of time before it strikes again!"

"It's not going to bite anyone, and he's not infected"

Everyone turned to old Hector.

He continued to speak, in his usual soft tones.

"I looked after Sonny for four-"...

He could see the interviewer's expression change.

"Sonny?"

He smiled shyly, "Yes, well that's what I named him when he used to come to my garage at night for his feed", he turned to the Monkey expert, "You probably won't believe me when I tell you that he exchanged gifts with me"

Benjamin Walsh just shook his head nonsensically.

"No, you're right, I don't"

The old man carried on with the unlikely scenario.

"In exchange for gifts of food, the little monkey would leave me parts that he had collected from motor cars parked nearby".

While Hector looked guiltily at the camera, knowing his neighbours now knew who and where, Mr. Walsh inhaled impatiently, pulling himself further up his chair.

"I don't know if you are aware, but you are sending out a very dangerous signal here, Mr...."

The interviewer and Hector both answered "Kerr" at the same time

"Mr. Kerr", he nodded, "What we have here is, an animal that is very capable of, in this instance, biting, and fatally infecting someone, a child even"

He sat forward in his chair, "This isn't some cute

organ grinders monkey we have here, but a streetwise beast, that will strike out and bite first, as in the case of the Police Officer, not so long ago!"

"He was drugged"

Now everyone turned to Harry.

"He was drugged?" asked the presenter, biting her lip anxiously.

Harry nodded.

"While they were trying to capture him, he was shot in the arm with a tranquillised dart, so Tawny wasn't quite who he should be"

"Tawny?"

For a fleeting moment, a smile crossed Harry's lips, but he spoke matter of factly.

"Yes, that's his name"

Gary looked in surprise to Terry, then both turned to old Hector.

The old man smiled easily to them, then mouthed, "I didn't know, did I?"

"His eyes were extremely large and deep when he was born, almost saucer like, so I christened him Tawny", he turned and smiled to the children, pulling his boot further up his lap, "After the owl"

The presenter fluttered hers, "Oh, I see".

"Have you ever been drugged, Mr. Walsh?"

Now everyone turned to the boy who addressed the monkey expert.

Gary.

Walsh looked uncomfortably from the boy to the interviewer.

She lifted her eyebrows... "Well?"

This made the expert inhale deeply before he

answered.

"No, I don't think so", he answered, very conscious of what he had to say.

"Not even in hospital?"

Gary.

The expert was then aware of everyone's eyes on him, and he could feel himself beginning to sweat.

He only shook his head and muttered "No"

Gary turned from him and addressed the rest of the group.

"Well I know that when I got my operation to get my hernia sorted, my Mammy say's that I was as high as a kite after it, and if wee Sonny felt anythi-", he turned guiltily toward Harry, "I'm sorry, if wee Tawny, felt anything like I felt, then I'm not surprised that he bit anyone after being shot and chased with the Police", the boy turned toward the presenter, shaking his head as he finished.

"I think I'd probably have done the same!"

Through her earphone, the presenter heard the director's voice, telling her to stop smiling so much at the boy.

"He's never been aggressive at all, he's just a wee softy"....

Now everyone turned to the boy who looked down to his feet as he spoke.

Terry.

"He stayed with me for two days, he even shared the same bed as me"

He looked up ruefully toward his mum, who stared dead ahead.

She seemed mortified at the news.

The rather dumbfounded interviewer took it from

there.

"What were your thoughts on the monkey Mrs. Connolly?"

"I had absolutely no thought at all on the monkey, I was never aware at any time, that it was in my house", she looked in some resignation over to her son, "But it does explain a few thing though"...

Terry shuffled his feet uncomfortably, then continued to look at them, as he spoke.

"We fed him, we took him to the forest and played all day with him", he looked awkwardly in his Mums direction for a second, then back to the floor, "we even shared the same food and drink", then an innocent smile broke across his face as he looked over to Harry, "Do you know he likes Peanut butter and jam sandwiches and cola?"

"No", he smiled wistfully, "But I'm not surprised"

"And penguin biscuits!" added Gary, then he sat forward and held his hand out to the interviewer.

"I've got some pictures of him, we took them back then"...

They were passed along and a camera zoomed in on them behind the presenter.

The first one showed Terry holding onto Chee, the monkey was restrained with a dog collar and extension lead.

The second showed Gary and Sonny.

The third showed both boys and Tawny, smiles beaming from the two mates back to the camera, as they held the monkey.

George Dunbar looked down to the television screen and made sure it was recording.

Then he smiled in supreme satisfaction.

The interviewer was trying not to smile as she handed them back, she looked over to the adults in the pro-monkey group.

"So are you suggesting that the monkey isn't dangerous, that it should be let go?"

Harry sat forward and licked his lips in deliberation.

"No, I'm not suggesting that we let Tawny loose", he shook his head quite profoundly, "No".

Then he looked toward the ape expert, "But I don't think he should be shot and killed, as we've all seen and heard, he isn't in the least violent or aggressive, and I really don't think that he's infected at all", he swept his hand around the group,

"None of us do!"

The expert was quite aghast!

This was his chance, his fifteen minutes of fame.

He wanted to be an Ape Expert on T.V.

But it was slipping through his fingers, like sand, he could feel it....

This was the most dangerous creature in the country, the potentially disease ridden Macaque, the scourge that he was warning the West of Scotland to avoid, at all costs.

There was danger of death here!!!!

There might have been the seeds of a career in television here!!!

Signs of death all around, and now, the huge television audience were being shown nice little family snaps of the wee monkey, out for a nice walk in the forest and holding hands with two lovely little boys!

It was all too much for him...

Then, fortunately for Mr. Walsh, the screen flicked to live pictures, covering the search for the monkey in the

Mall.

The beast was spotted on the roof of the Cinema, and the forces at hand were closing in.

Chapter 33

Race for Life!

The Policeman was quite literally frozen in shock when the monkey appeared in his sight.

With fur blackened and soiled with oils and greases from its exploits in the darkened bowels of the building. The macaques teeth were bared as his eyes were held closed, burnt by the daylight after the full day spent in the darkness, he now looked the part of the blighted and disease ravaged beast that had been shown in the newspapers and television newscasts throughout the country over the last few days.

This sickly-looking apparition would have pleased the monkey expert, for the first few seconds the man's body went into an uncanny, spasmodic rigour. This was the reason the first burst of bullets went well wide of him, smashing and thudding into the brickwork and flat rooftop around him. Tiny shards of brickwork and red-hot metal ricocheted around the monkey's head and sent him racing across the rooftop in an effort to escape the man, who then communicated feverishly through a hand-held radio.

Then the force came together, alerted and moving as one to the west end of the complex, just above the giant twelve screened cinema where the beast was now headed.

Twenty-five armed Officers dispatched with clear orders to kill the beast on the first sight of it. Now with all arms pointed in the rooftops direction, crouched and poised, they were ready to fire whenever the macaque came into their sights.

But there was no sight.

The multi-blocked mall was a combination of many different buildings, mostly flat topped but some of the roofs were apex in design, these were built later than the original and as the monkey jumped from level to level, more shots rung out from the distance. Thankfully they whizzed over his head or thudded into the ground and walls around him. His getaway from the humans was erratic, he bolted away from the direction that the shots had come from, and whenever they zapped on the wall and floor, he zigzagged manically away, point to point from them, high above the waiting response unit. Three humans had fired from three directions around him but they were now aware that there were crossfire implications; consequently they held their fire. The little monkey waited, hiding just below the ridge of a two-foot high brick wall. He could hear their gathering footsteps on the roofs surrounding him; he pulled his trembling body down further into the wall and gasped for air. He looked down and noticed patches of blood on the soles of his feet and palms of his hands, cut and scored from jumping into the pebble-dashed buildings. No one had seen the macaque leave the west wing; three Officers were now behind him and worked their way along, pointing their rifle barrels into any places that the beast may be hiding.

Ready to shoot first, no questions would be asked.

The outside broadcast units were beaming the pictures live to the West of Scotland television audience, drop-jawed families watched the scene in amazement, dinners in laps and cutlery frozen in their hands. An on the spot reporter spoke over the amazing pictures as the Policemen waited to pounce on the little animal, around the deserted cinema.

Everyone's eyes were drawn to the cinemas high apex roof, and then the watching masses could se the monkey work his way to the highest point of the mall. The television audience watched breathlessly on as the beast clambered along the roofs peak and then pulled himself across it. All the time studiously watching down to all below him. After some tense moments a single shot rang out but it was deflected by the sloping roof and spun high over his head. This made it retreat back the way and everyone watched it as it clambered along the apex of the roof, then slither back down on the blind side, and again disappear into the mass of rooftops around him.

Then the hunt was thrown into overdrive when a shout was heard from the rear end of the cinema, the macaque was descending a drainpipe and into the rear car park. Most of the force had gathered at the front of the building so it took a mad dash to get there just as the monkey leapt the last few feet down and thudded onto the concrete below him.

He ran toward the sanctity of a few parked motorcars which still lay in the car park. They provided him with some cover to escape the posse which just rounded the corner. At that point the little beast looked frantically around itself for the forest which would provide salvation, but he had come down on the far side of the mall from where he had entered the supermarket, this area was heavily built up and gave little chance of escape for him.

Ten humans rounded the corner from one side, then eight from the other, all moving quickly and stealthily, rifles and handguns pointed ahead. The first one on the spot yelled to the rest as they came upon the scene.

"IT'S IN THERE, AMONG THE CARS!"

They slowly made to round the small allotment of cars, then saw the beast break cover and run toward the car park exit.

A huge volley of gunfire was released into the space the monkey ran toward, car windscreens were shattered, tyres popped lifelessly flat, and bullets thudded into the sides of the empty vehicles around him, but miraculously, the beast kept on running!

The team then ran ahead and followed, firing sporadically at it, and watching in disbelief as it rounded the corner and disappeared momentarily out of their sight.

Pursuers now gathered from all directions, Policemen and on the spot report news teams now included, and as they rounded the corner they came upon the sight of the overspill carpark, where their own emergency and personal vehicles sat, parked.

Over fifty irregularly parked motorcars, vans and lorries sitting in no particular order.

They moved quickly to surround the area and cut off any means of the macaque escaping.

Two men at each corner of the lot, watching for any movement from it, the teams started to work their way along the length of the park, carefully checking underneath each of the parked vehicles.

They stood well clear as two officers inspected the underside, again holding the rifle barrels protectively forward, but there was the ever present danger of crossfire casualties and the constant danger of exploding fuel tanks, detonated by a carelessly discharged bullet, so there was a note of extreme caution as they made their was along the ranks of vehicles.

Thirteen cars and vans, all checked and clear.

The suspense heightened, each of the inspecting officers were weighed down with constricting uniforms, hats, thick gloves and masks, all protection from a possible bite, clawing or spit from the ravaged beast.

Then a whispered shout emerged from the far side of the lot.

An officer indicated by pointing, that he had come across something. He stood back and waited at the scene, rifle pointed expectantly at the vehicle before him, as his colleagues gathered around him.

Without speaking, he pointed to a small trail of blood-smudged paw prints on the bonnet of a car. They led to the roof of a people carrier, then he indicated the vehicle it sat next to.

The Television Company's high-sided van, festooned with aerials, cables and satellite dishes.

Ladders were attached to the side and rear of the vehicle.

The leader of the force looked over to the nearest uniformed Officer.

Then he pointed his rifle from him, to the top of the vehicle.

The Officer walked quickly forward, and then grasped the rung on the ladder at the rear of the van, and then he slowly started to climb.

In moments the vehicle was completely surrounded and each of the force had a weapon pointed at the rooftop.

Everyone almost held their breath during the tension filled moments that it took for the Officer to climb the ladder, with every slow, deliberate step he took, the pressure around the parking lot seemed to rise agonisingly.

His head came level with the rooftop of the van.

From that level, he looked down toward his commander, and again without words, indicated that he could see nothing.

The commander nodded him upward; he could see boxes attached, storage units, which the animal may use to conceal itself from them.

The officer lifted his head again and breathing very heavily by this time, raised himself and climbed cautiously onto the roof.

Now each one of the force watching, took a step back for a clearer aim, but their commander waved his hand and silently tried to calm them a little, while the man on the roof of the van approached the storage units with growing apprehension. He walked as far out to the side of the vans walkway as he could.

Around the first unit was clear...

He approached the next, by this time the tension around the car lot was electrifying, each person knew that this was the beleaguered beast's last hiding place and would soon either bolt from the rooftop, or attack their colleague on the top of the vehicle.

The watching nation were glued to their television sets, not daring to take their eyes from it for a second, this had been a masterstroke, an absolute gift by the planners, to get the children and the other monkey sympathisers on the interview earlier, now it was paying, they were watching in untold droves.

Millions hopefully!

Officer Edward MacLean edged his way carefully toward the last rooftop storage box.

For five years he had waited for a situation as this, now,

he wasn't sure he could handle it.

Maybe the mad beast would attack and bite, he hoped his protective gear was as protective as it should be.

Or maybe even hit by a stray bullet from the hail of gunfire that he fully expected, he felt trails of sweat on the inside of his mask, beading, then forming small rivers of biting perspiration. It stung his face and distorted his sight, so much so, he felt like tearing it away and scratching his face off.

But he couldn't.

The tormented officer slowly rounded the corner of the last storage unit, and then thanked the Lord, the unit was clear!!!

He went to turn to his superior, but noticed the PVC flap, hanging loosely around it. He pointed his rifle anxiously toward it, he prepared for fire and aimed the rifle at the front of the box.

The staff in the immediate line of his fire were moved back from the front of the van, he inhaled slowly, staring in full intent to the box, and then held his breath!

The unit was blasted with the salvo of gunfire, fifteen twenty two-millimetre bullets thudded and crashed into the macaques lair, soon the box was a broken shell, smashed and shattered beyond any recognition or further use.

He started breathing again, inhaling heavily as he looked down to the shattered remains of the unit. He nodded to himself in nervous satisfaction, and then to the force that waited open-mouthed almost, directly below him.

He edged forward and slowly lifted the remnants of the flap with his rifle barrel.

He shook his head.....

Unbelievingly...

He lifted the flap further, and delved the rifle nozzle further in, pulling broken cables, connectors and smashed monitors from the box.

But no Macaque!!

He yelled from the top of his lungs to his leader.

"THERE'S NOTHING UP HERE SIR!"

And just as the bewildered force started to look confusingly around themselves, the monkey broke from the underside of the vehicle, startled from his hideaway by the rapid burst of shattering gunfire.

Then he was haring away again, an officer lined up his rifle and had the monkey easily in his sights.

He coolly squeezed on the trigger, then held back in horror as he saw a colleague directly opposite, him also ready to open fire.

Both men lifted their rifles carefully into the air, then the macaque channelled into more cars and ran directly toward the main road, the railway station, and the town centre hubbub!

The force following the monkey ran in three separate groups not far behind him. They were now heading for a very public area, the town centre, so they were ordered to hold fire until further instructed.

Only a drugged dart would be allowed now, but the monkey didn't know that.

Still terrified witlessly, huge, featureless buildings, now surrounded him and ran for as long as he could see.

Great motor vehicles thundered and screeched to a halt along the main road, and people, now bewildered totally by the sight that the whole country had been talking over for the past two days, stopped and watched on open-mouthed as the procession bundled along the length of the main road!

Chee had no option but to keep running, but by this time his lungs were struggling to give him the strength to keep his wearied and almost jellified little body going. He jumped, thumped and trundled his way along, through the absolutely amazed town-centre rush hour, and even though he appeared to be dying on his feet, amazingly, he seemed to be at least keeping his distance from his pursuers.

He ran down a gap in the brickwork that appeared in the buildings, and then found himself running down a long sloping footpath, that a few astonished people walked along.

By now, most people had heard and spoke of the potentially disease ridden macaque, remembering the huge pictures that had headlined the Daily Nationals two days since, he was recognised in most cases instantly. Everyone that was in the macaques path seemed to be horrified as the beast sped toward them, all pulling themselves anxiously to the side of the walkway, desperate to let the notorious beast speed past them!

Chee was totally unaware that he was headed for the railway line, all he could see was a swath of greenbelt in the distance, the salvation of the countryside, and deliverance from the chasing humans to the sanctity of the forested countryside, looked to be only a few frantic moments from him!

In seconds he heard the pack behind him round the corner, then clatter down the path toward him.

There were no trains on the line as the monkey hurtled toward it.

Watched from behind, the simian arrived at the platform then leapt forward and up, from the stage of the platform, to the overhead power-lines above him.

There was a sudden, blinding flash; a terrible vision of smoke and bilious white steam filled the air over the rail lines.

The force stopped and watched helplessly, as a sickening scream echoed around the station, then the body that they had tried to detect and capture for the past two days, the little monkey that most of the country had been scared senseless from, was finally thrown down, and left to them from the power-lines above.

It landed in a crumpled, lifeless heap, still smoking and steaming pitifully, fifteen feet from the platform.

Chapter 34

Goodbye...

Old men and women.

Commuting workers of all ages.

Mothers and Fathers with their children.

School-kids.

All shuffling forward for a last, unbelieving look at it...

Time seemed to freeze, then slowly inch past, as each one edged slowly to the rim of the platform, or as close as they were allowed by the Policemen who tried to move them on and away, assuring them that there was nothing more to see.

To see it...

Sadly, it was all over...

Now most of the watching public had a hollow-eyed, and distraught look about them as they watched and whispered quietly, at the scene of the little monkeys end.

Even some of the Police men and women were quite saddened after witnessing the monkey's electrocution.

The body lay where it fell, and the sobering station was slowly cleared.

There would be no trains running in the meantime, the overhead power lines were isolated and switched off until the body was removed.

They moved out slowly, in sad lines.

People were moved and somehow captivated by the little beasts tragic plight, it could never have know, it could never win.

Then without any word or warning, someone jumped from the masses at the platform edge and landed noisily on the shale surrounding the tracks.

He then proceeded to trudge through the stones, over to the lifeless body.

Three Policemen immediately moved to the edge of the platform and bawled at him.

"WILL YOU COME BACK HERE SIR, NO ONE IS ALLOWED THERE!"

Through narrow slits of eyes, the beast's keeper, Harry Ramsay stared bitterly up at them and then tramped beyond them.

One of the Policemen recognised him, then spoke no more.

No-one in the massed platform spoke, but watched silently on as the Keeper slowly peeled off his old leather jacket and stood over the carcass.

He then carefully laid the garment over the little beasts still body.

He knelt down beside it for a few silent seconds, one hand on the macaques body, the other cupping his head, in thought.

He then reflected for a moment upon the terrified little alien beast, in a land so alien to it.

The poor little sap, never understood for a second what he had got himself into.

"Goodbye Tawny, hope you're where you'd like to be…

He tapped the body gently and then stood up and went to go and leave the last remnant of his little tribe of macaques that had been with him for the past twenty years...

Chapter 35

Nature's Way.

Most of the country had witnessed the electrocution that evening.

Live.

The televised pictures were transmitted on the Scottish News at six o'clock, then the national News at 10.

Most were sympathetic with his case, for now the mood of the nation was of pity for the sad little beast, rather than the terrible hysterics before.

Terry and Gary, old Hector and the Muir girls and Harry, his keeper, had managed to persuade the nation that the monkey was no real danger, the expert just seemed to melt away, relieved his fifteen minutes of fame, or infamy, were now over.

Terry and Gary knew they would never be the same, they would always have this terrible soft spot for the bravest and cheekiest of monkeys, his giant newspaper front page adorned each of their bedrooms.

The Muir ladies were saddened also, Lorna-Ann had the same front page framed and mounted, as did a substantial proportion of the nation's kids.

Old Hector was just so sad it had to happen, but in a way he had always feared the worst for his little Sonny, but he couldn't have dreamed as tragic an end as this.

And Harry.

Fortunately, Harry didn't have too much time to dwell on the past, the parks authorities had decided to renew their colony of Rhesus and most of the next days were spent readying the huts for their new occupants, twenty four charges were being prepared from different locations across Europe and the U.K. and although he couldn't get the image and memories of a gutsy little beast named Tawny from his mind, it was now time to think and plan for the future.

He had to be positive, for all of their collective sakes.

Each of the old huts were demolished and burnt, the whole area was painstakingly and scientifically cleaned and new living and sleeping quarters were to be rebuilt. All kinds of preparation work was taking place on the site of the old colonies enclosure. His whole next three weeks were to be spent busily preparing for their arrival.

Soon enough new life would replace the old, it's quite sad and brutal sometimes, but Harry knew, it is nature's way.

He had a wry smile on his face that evening as he quite wearily sat back on his armchair, just about to eat his dinner.

Would these next troops present him with car parts as the last ones?

Would they be part-time charmers and full-time fitters, as the last troops?

Tawny and his brother Simon.

Mary, Una, Basil and Sam.

Terry, Ailsa and Heinz.

He smiled at the thought of them as he picked up the ringing telephone.

"Yes, speaking"

He didn't speak for almost a full half- minute, physically, he couldn't!

He grunted out a name and address, repeating it while he wrote it down.

Then he left his home.

He arrived in Glasgow, thirty-five minutes later...

Harry approached the dimly lit four-story building and swallowed uncomfortably as he passed the sign.

THE SCOTTISH CENTRE FOR ANIMAL HUSBANDRY AND FIELD RESEARCH.

A Government sign lay under the notice.

Security cameras monitored the entrance vestibule, he watched it while he pressed the buzzer and waited for entry. After a few moments, the door clicked and fell open.

A white-coated female stood on the other side, smiling skittishly.

Quite pretty and in her mid-twenties, her eyebrows raised hopefully as she spoke to him.

"Mister Ramsay?"

He nodded, an uncomfortable half-smile on his lips also.

"Yes"

She looked around herself, and then stood back, beckoning him forward into the brightly lit corridor as she spoke.

"Mister Ramsay, I'm Sandra Macdonald, would you like to come this way?"

He nodded and followed her. She walked quickly ahead of him, so much so her white coat seemed to flap in the light breeze as she whizzed along, he had to walk a little faster than usual just to keep up with her. She checked around herself, and as she spoke, she seemed to him to be a rather nervous person.

"Just up three flights of stairs Mister Ramsay", she held the stairway door open for him, still looking suspiciously around the area. "Harry", he half-smiled, "Just call me Harry"

She smiled shyly, and started to climb the stairs.

"I don't think we should use the lift at all Harry, there's still staff around, a late meeting was called for tonight, I think they want to congratulate themselves and pat their own backs with their apparent success in dealing with the S.H. virus", she looked wearily behind herself to him.

"But we know better"

Harry's mind raced almost as quickly as Sandra's legs as they climbed the stairs, surely not?

They sped up the two remaining flights of concrete steps, and then she stood at the door and peered through a tiny opening.

"We need to be very careful now, if we're found out here there's going to be questions asked, never mind what we've got in 27c"

They both walked quickly down the corridor, her sometimes breaking into a slight trot. There were no signs of life at this level of the Government run building, the lights were dimmed and set to low level. They travelled the whole length of the passage, and then she stopped and stood at a large wooden door.

It was marked 27c

She tapped it softly, looking around for a last time, and then she spoke quietly into it.

"Holly, it's only me, Sandra

She turned and smiled hopefully to Harry.

They heard a click from inside the door.

A plump, middle-aged lady pulled the door open in a flash, then ushered the other two quickly through.

"Hurry, come through!"

Both rushed in then it was quietly closed and locked behind them.

Harry just stood at the door and looked around himself.

He seemed to be in some kind of laboratory, there were all kinds of machines and monitors, electrical gadgets attached with tubes and wires led into glass cases.

Some had animals lying inside, in all cases they seemed to be asleep.

Or...

In all, it seemed a cold, sterile environment.

Sandra turned to the older lady and spoke.

"How is he?"

She clasped her hands hopefully.

Her older friends face broke into a soft grin, "He's fine, he's just the same as when you left!"

Sandra turned to Harry, holding his hand gently as she spoke to him.

"Harry, I want to introduce you to Holly, without her help it would have been impossible, he'd never have made it!"

The older girl shook her head nonsensically and smiled warmly to him.

"Holly, this is Harry, Harry, this is Holly!"

They all smiled at the play on words.

"Harry, I'm pleased to meet you, would you like to come over and see him, I'll bet your dying to!"

He smiled in return and nodded, but he still couldn't believe it!

He had seen it, he had witnessed the little beast's electrocution, he had seen its lifeless body left on the tracks, surely it couldn't have survived that?!

They walked through the large studio, he noticed rabbits, mice and rats in different cages and glass cases as they went the length of the room, again, most seemed asleep but he didn't know, they could have been drugged, or, whatever....

He shivered inwardly, contemplating the animal's eventual fates.

They stopped at the end of the room in a dimly lit corner and the ladies stood by a small glass door, about the size of a small fridge.

There, with pipes leading into the cage and through a swath of bandages, he could see the little monkey.

Swaddled with plasters and dressings, and with tubes inserted into his arm and nostrils, the macaque he knew as Tawny, lay sleeping inside the case, on a bed of a thick, woollen blanket.

A six-inch cuddly monkey toy lay at the foot of the case, propped up against his paws.

He turned and smiled unbelievably to them.

"How the hell could he have survived such a shock? I saw it happen, he was literally fried!"

Sandra turned to Holly; they both had broad grins on their faces.

Holly spoke first.

"What we have here is a quite remarkable little beast, Mister Ramsay, this little lad will just not give in!" she smiled as she explained further, "You obviously thought he was done for, and you covered him with your jacket"

She pointed to it hanging on the wall rack.

"But in a funny way, it was probably that very action which saved his life!"

They were all looking into the case as she continued.

Harry shook his head in uncertainty as he remembered the event.

"If the Police or the Health boys had come across him before you?"

She raised a suspicious eyebrow during the explanation.

"They would have checked him" she looked fearfully over her specs to Sandra, "And we all know what would have happened then, don't we?!"

The three nodded, still gazing into the case.

"He was stuck ingloriously into a black bin bag, and then Sandra's friend from the R.S.P.C.A. was called over to dispose of the body" she turned toward him and grued.

"By incineration"...

Harry found this sight before him almost impossible to take in; he kept shaking his head in disbelief, then re-belief, a haunting half-smile set on his face.

"Schoolchildren have survived electric shocks on railway lines too Harry", added Holly, "It does happen, you know!"

He gulped air just before he spoke. It was a minor miracle that the little beast had survived this much, but one question remained unanswered. He lifted his hand to his jaw as he spoke.

"And what about... the virus?".....

"I'll let you tell him this Sandra, after all, this is your field!"

Sandra held his fingers again, smiling to him and looking over her glasses as she spoke.

"Your little friend didn't have the virus Harry, he was never infected at any point!"

"We were right?!"...he half-whispered.

"Yes, you were right!"

He felt like telling the world!

He felt like getting the monkey expert, Mr. Walsh, and personally dragging him here, to be told the fantastic news, then back onto National Television, and screaming it into his face!

Tawny was clear, and the best part of thirty Police men and women and Government Health troopers, had tried to detect, then eliminate him.

And they had failed, they had all failed!!

With all their weapons, guns and gadgetry, they had failed!!!

He looked satisfyingly into the case and spoke through what felt like a twelve-inch grin!

"So how is he, what's the prognosis?"

Holly nodded down satisfactorily toward the beast and pointed out his injuries.

"He has burns and lesions on his front paws, a slight graze where I think a bullet must have grazed him and nipped into his ribs, and most of his hair is singed off." She smiled at the thought of the near hairless monkey, "It will grow back in time, and all told, he's going to pull through, he is, as I've said, one remarkable little beast, he just doesn't know how to give in!"

The ladies made Harry some tea at nine, he just sat and wondered how two females who must nullify the lives of countless animals on an annual basis in the laboratory, could risk everything, to save a distressed little simian.

He truly marvelled at them both.

They spoke at length about Tawny and the colonies of Rhesus that were culled in Scotland, England and Wales, a total of over four hundred macaques. The ladies could see that it still hurt Harry to speak of them, but now there was comfort and great hope for the future with Tawny's unbelievable escape from death, he smiled down to the case.

Harry then remembered the greatest escapologist of all time, and reflected.

"I should have named him Houdini, never mind Tawny!"

"Or Sonny", smiled Sandra, "He was clear from the virus, he couldn't have known, but his escape from the sanctuary had proved to be the very action that has saved his life!"

Sandra and Harry both nodded in dawning realisation of the fact, agreeing with Holly's statement.

"Jeez!" added Harry, "He should have been born a cat!"

Both ladies smiled at the thought, and Sandra added, "Yes, nine lives, and all that!"

They all smiled together and looked back in great happiness, to the near hairless, four-named monkey that should have been born a cat!

And named Houdini!!!

Chapter 36

The New Intake – Sareen.

Three weeks had passed and in that time everyone was kept busy.

Harry was heavily involved in the acceptance routines of the new troop of macaques, and the restructuring of their new living quarters. Eight males and six females, all fully developed, and a mixture of eight other younger monkeys, from only a few months old to just under full development.

Berra and Chee monkeys.

In the three weeks, Tawny, or Sonny, or Squeaky or Chee, had recovered well from his terrible ordeal. The scars on his hands and arms had almost healed, the little nick on his side was more superficial than anything else, and his fur had yet to fully grow back in, but he was doing very well and better than anyone could have hoped for in the private sanctuary which was his secret recovering home for the present.

But his personality had also seemed to have changed, for most of the time he sat in his little hut, or in the furthest reaches of his outdoor run, watching every movement that was made by his human carers with unrelenting suspicion.

He had no idea why he was being held there, something in his mind suggested that he had seen Har-ree, but it was all part of a terrible dream sequence which grew fainter as each day passed.

He had no recollection of the electrocution; he only remembered a bright blinding flash, and then?

So he watched this new band of humans through lowered and suspicious eyes, they seemed to be kind and friendly, but so were the young humans he had befriended and looked after him all those days ago, and look what had happened after that.

He was taken to a safe refuge in the Borders, where he was expected to recover fully.

But his future was uncertain.

It was impossible to let him back into the Safari Park as things stood, for as a direct consequence of the Simian herpes scare, all monkeys in the park were to be given an identity and health check in the incoming days, their health was to be monitored on a more regular basis than before, and at this point there was documentation for only twenty four monkeys in the enclosures.

His presence was still unknown to but a few informed and well-meaning sympathisers.

Still, no one out of the ring of confidant's was aware that the beast had survived, and was clear of any disease, and had been all along. This would be a public relations disaster to the big boys in the Public Health Department, wings would be clipped and careers would be curtailed if it was revealed that people in the very department that was ordered to stamp out its very existence, had actually aided and abetted the monkey's recovery!

So it was decided it would be best all round if he was hidden until a place was made available with a like-minded establishment.

The new colony of Rhesus had arrived and it had only taken days for them to start building their own social order.

A lone male had started to acquire females for his

harem, in mind and body he was easily the strongest and most intelligent of the troop, and other, weaker members had become unwilling underlings, eating and drinking only after he had satisfied himself fully.

Harry was a little dismayed the way their days seemed to be panning out, indolence seemed to be the order of their particular day. Unlike the last industrious families that had been in the park, they spent their time resting and eating, then sleeping long into the day.

Occasionally the leader, arriving from Belgium and with the name of Bower, would erupt with another male, usually at feeding times or with females present.

Harry knew well that this was mostly for show, the leader always had to keep tabs on any up and coming males with growing ambitions and although there were none that came near him here, he stood on anything anyway.

Bower kept two fawning individual males as subordinates, and they were well satisfied at being second, and third in line from him. Privately, both dreamed that one day their time would come but at this point, they kept their ambitions well under wraps.

But something happened in the park, something which would again change Chee's life, so completely.

Gentle activity around his pen alerted him early one morning, he peered around the opening and viewed the humans outside.

Two men called for him, using the name that Har-ree had given him.

Tawny.

They entered the pen and closed the grilled door behind them, both gently whispering the name.

"Tawny, Tawny"

Chee immediately rushed to the gnarled formation of logs which led to the top of the covered pen, and after scurrying to the top, he watched them guardedly.

He sat his ground and waited till they approached.

Then the simian found himself as if possessed, he screamed wildly at the two men, then leapt to the other side of the run, while the men looked on in confusion.

All the time the monkey's heart and lungs thumped and pumped heavily inside him.

They left the pen but returned after a few moments with nets attached to long, looping poles.

The monkey was then gathered, his claws flailing wildly, snapping his jaws at the handlers and screaming for all that he was worth.

Before too long he was captured then he was stowed into a transit cage and packed into a waiting van.

A space had become available, and of all the places that the covenant of friends and like-minded colleagues had discussed that may become suitable for him, from wildlife parks and private collections throughout the British Isles.

A space had become available in the great Safari-Park in Stirling.

The very one he had escaped from all those months earlier.

A year-old male had died due to injuries inflicted after a fight with another male.

This had never happened before in all the time that Harry had spent in the park. He had found the dying macaque during his early morning check and had called in the vet, but sadly the beast succumbed after only a few hours. He wasn't witness to the attack and was unaware that the mortal injuries it had received during the attack and prolonged mauling, were from Bower and the two other lead males.

Unfortunately Harry couldn't have known whatever happened behind the closed doors of the huts, and couldn't see the extent of the bullying and harrying over food and position which was taking place.

And now Chee was being brought to this scene, the place where two male macaques strode around like lords and where one acted as the very king, giving orders over who ate, breathed, lived and slept in the tiny, sorry enclave that was now their home.

If they could bring him in and assimilate him with the others then they could hopefully pass him off as the macaque that had passed away, full medical and insertion of registration chips was only a few days off, so it was vital to get him in to the park and its new ways as soon as possible.

He was transported to the park at six-thirty that morning.

His cage was lifted from the van to a park open vehicle, he was thankful when he first heard, then saw, Har-ree. The vehicle then drove toward the macaque enclosure.

All the time that the cage was being transported, he watched unbelievably out toward the familiar, yet very unfamiliar landscape.

There was an eerie, unearthly strangeness about the place he used to know as home.

Macaques started to run and howl alongside the flatbed that transported his cage inside the grounds.

He was in shock, he recognized no one!

He inhaled long and thoughtful breaths of the parks new air, it soon became terribly apparent to him.

These were not his friends and family, the macaques gathering around and hooting into the blue sky were totally unfamiliar to him.

His cage was lifted and taken to the last hut, which didn't seem to be getting used much, all the time Harry tried talking to and soothing the beasts which crowded around him and the cage he lifted in. It was as if the other animals demanded to know the identity of this interloper, but Chee's troubles hadn't even started with the new family of macaques.

He was watched from the other side of the monkeys range.

Bower stood, proud and erect, his chest puffed and his head lifted into the air.

He sniffed and grimaced at the strange and strong incoming scent.

Male...

He spat!

Fully grown...

He spat again, wilfully into the ground, and as he stretched up fully his hackles rose.

He called his cohorts to accompany him.

Then he strode over to investigate.

Chee could see he had returned home, but he had never felt so alone or alienated in his life.

Har-ree and another human had brought him into the new hut, but left after a few minutes, leaving him still inside his cage. But for that he could be thankful, he watched on in stunned silence while other macaques walked around the cage, trying to sniff, pick, scratch and goad him into some kind of action.

They didn't speak like him; he struggled to understand what they were saying.

One jumped forward and bellowed to him.

"Who are you, you smell like a forest pig!"

He tried to grab a handful of Chee's fur but he pulled himself into the centre of his cage. Another stretched his arm from the other side and nipped his fur; Chee turned feverishly around and swiped to clear the paw.

"Hey! You smack my hand! I get the master to get you like he did the last one!"

Chee stared across to him with bared teeth.

"You get sorted the way Chian got sorted, you see!"

Then he spat into the cage.

A youngster ran forward and pushed a stick into the cage, hitting Chee's legs with it.

He just stood and watched the child without speaking or breaking from his frown.

Then he heard the deep, thunderous voice breaking through the din made by the pack which surrounded the cage.

"INTRUDER IN MY AREA!" it roared, "WHO ARE YOU!?"

Chee turned around and lifted his head nervously.

He inhaled deeply when he looked to the far side of the hut. This was the first sighting of the leader of this new troop; he knew that eventually he would have to battle with him when this cage was opened, as he knew it would be. He could see two morons smiling stupidly by his side, he knew then he could never win the forthcoming confrontation, but that wouldn't stop it from happening.

It shouted again as it slowly walked forward.

"TRESPASSER, I ASK YOU AGAIN, WHO ARE YOU!"

Chee almost felt he couldn't speak, his stomach churned as the lead macaques voice filled the room. His jaw trembled as he spoke.

"I'm a Chee monkey from this area...

The macaque known as Bower looked incredulously from Chee, then cast his gaze to the silenced masses.

His face broke into a cruel smile as he mimicked his captive's voice.

"YOU'RE A CHEE MONKEY- FROM THIS AREA?!"

The two other fools started giggling inanely, and then the audience laughed along with them.

Bower turned mightily from them, leered hatefully into the cage, and then he bawled toward Chee.

"YOU ARE NO CHEE MONKEY FROM THIS AREA! THIS IS MY AREA, YOU HEAR ME!"

Bower leapt forward and threw himself at the cage, stretching inside. As he did so his stooges screamed and hollered along with him. The hut was soon filled with the cacophonous roars of twenty three delirious macaques, each one bawling along as their leader and his followers attempted to get access to the trespasser, and tried to get their claws into him, the intruder.

The shrieking, screaming, yelling and crying only stopped when Harry re-entered the hut.

The monkeys ran from the centre of the shelter and stood around the edges, revealing the reason for their dislike.

The cage was upended and lying upside down, five

yards from where it was first laid.

He could see Tawny, winded, battered and bruised and just starting to pull himself from the floor.

Harry tried to reassure the winded monkey while he straightened the cage.

"You'll be alright son, you'll find your place in this group as the last", he comforted himself with the words more than the stricken monkey while he stretched in and patted the macaques head.

"It just might take a wee bit of time, that's all"...

Chapter 37

The Dream.

Chee looked from the floor to the area around himself. He watched another, a Chee female approach and walk purposefully past the cage. A much younger monkey appeared to bump against her, pitching her against the cage. She shook her head in annoyance with the infant.

"Tinu!"

He looked back to her, in complete surprise almost.

The female shook her head impatiently, telling the young beast he should be a little more careful, and then walked off.

She looked into his cage as she moved away.

He thought she had the most wonderful brown monkey eyes he had ever seen, staring at him through the guddle of monkeys and steel bars around him.

Chee looked toward her, but then her sight dropped to the floor of the cage.

She nodded down for him to look.

He took his sight from her, then down.

A half-banana! He held his breath in uncertainty.

He looked back up to her, and then she nodded him on again.

She mimicked and mouthed that he should eat it!

Chee picked it up, she eyed the hut suspiciously to make sure she hadn't been spotted feeding the intruder, and then she exited the hut.

He stayed in the cage for the remainder of the afternoon, picked, pushed, pulled at and goaded all day, until at last; they seemed to tire of it. Then at the end of the late afternoon the keeper Har-ree entered the huts and started to feed the animals. He approached the cage while the rest were being fed and watered, then he unlocked it.

Chee allowed Harry to pull him out, the keeper rubbing the monkey's head affectionately and speaking the unknown human language while he was petted. The keeper then exited the hut, pulling the empty cage out with him.

With the cage, he had taken Chee's last form of protection, and from then on in, he waited for it.

He was left to sit in the middle of the floor of the hut where the younger and much smaller monkeys were allowed to continue with their open goading of him as they walked around him.

They very publicly insulted him.

He smelled like a forest hog.

He was ugly and spoke like a foreigner.

"Like a foreign hog!"

He closed his eyes in dread when he saw Bower enter the hut with his cronies, and as he expected, they made straight for him.

"Intruder, you out of the hard-hut now!"...

Chee tried to swallow but his throat remained bone-dry.

He only nodded while he stared submissively down to the floor, he felt he couldn't return Bowers imperious gaze.

That would mean a challenge.

"What are you going do now you're not hidden from me?"

He could only whisper a reply, still looking shamefully down at his feet and away from the arrogant Bower.

"Nothing"...

He could feel Bowers eyes on him, beading down from

above as he sat on the floor.

Then Chee quite literally saw stars, he was beaten on the side of the head and was pulled upward by the scruff of his neck as he tried to recover from it.

He could feel the prodigious strength of the great beasts forearms lifting him upward as he was pulled level with him.

Then the great macaque spat into his face, holding him by the scruff of his neck and warning him with a fixed and resolute stare.

"IF I SEE ONE LOOK FROM YOU, JUST ONE TIME YOUR EYE'S CATCH MINE!", saliva speckled Chee's face as the lead monkey barked his chilling warning to the new member of the troop. He shook his head submissively, still avoiding Bowers terrible, flaring eyes, still trying to stop his head from spinning with the full force of the savage blow.

He was slapped again on the side of his head, and then thrown to the floor with his head still spinning. They all spent the next few moments laughing and smiling amongst themselves, at the intruders long deserved welcome, and come-uppance!

But, he had to be thankful.

If this was the welcome by the leader of the new troop to an outsider, an intruder, then he was lucky. Not that he was aware, but considering the death in the camp the few days ago, he had got off lightly, very lightly.

"You last to eat and drink!" he was told, "Always last, remember that!"

And he did.

He never ate at all until the adult and children monkeys had had their fill, sometimes there would be only a scraping of food left when the sun had started to dip below the trees, and sometimes nothing. Soon weight began to fall from him, from being looked after and getting physically built up in the recovering home in the Borders, almost like royalty, he now ate and lived like a true pauper.

"Like a forest pig!"

At times he was unconscious of himself watching the others eat and had started to pick up and eat half-eaten scraps and dog ends of food they would leave down, such a dramatic change in so short a space of time. His heart was at its lowest ebb possible and he could see no end to the way things were in the park, the new park. The mysterious disappearance of his Mother, brother and the family of macaques would come and drape itself over him like a cloud and haunt him, and he would spend moments in desperate isolated depression, wondering.

It was as though someone had come and stolen his past from him.

He chose to spend most of his time in the hut where Har-ree had left him. Still constantly harangued and harried whenever he stepped outside, his existence seemed a little more bearable indoors away from the threat of Bower, his allies and their harem of females and younger ones who now had something that was lower in stature and stock than themselves. He shared the hut with some older macaques and others of lower esteem that had been delegated to this area before him.

Day turned slowly into evening, almost eventless apart from nipping and goading from other younger ones, and once again, more or less foodless.

He had been without sustenance for almost two days

from the lines of her palm and fingers. He held her hands and felt emotion beyond description; an enormous weight seemed lifted from him as someone showed care and compassion to him for the first time in this new and very strange family.

He cried into them, speaking lowly into her fingers.

"Thank you for showing me this kindness, you have no idea what your act means to me in this place"

He watched her silhouetted shape in the dimness of the hut while she replied.

"I had to help, to do something, you have went through so much, as Chian did"

He nodded unknowingly.

"Who was... Chian?"

"Chian was taken a time ago at Bowers hands, I thought and hoped so much"...

Then she started to weep softly.

"No, don't cry"

He could see her body begin to shake with emotion, she lifted a hand and covered her eyes.

"I watched them bring in with the hard house and hoped so much it was my older brother, Chian, brought home and recovered"...

Then Chee understood it was him and not her brother.

He continued to hold her hand.

"I'm sorry about Chian, if ever I can do anything to help your great sorrow over the loss of your brother"...

A motor vehicle rumbled past and she withdrew quickly from him.

"Female!" he gasped.

She turned, as she was about to exit the hut.

"What do I call you?"

now, and he lay in the darkened depression of the hut, struggling to find the contentment of sleep. The others around him were beginning to breathe heavily, and moan slightly into the beginnings of theirs.

He felt a nudge on him as he tried to fall over, but ignored it, now he was so used to it.

Then again, moments later.

He only lifted an eyelid from his wearying ball of half-sleep and spoke, weakened by hunger and now only half conscious. He mumbled through crusty lips.

"You must go back to sleep with your mother, it's very late, the shee-har will come for you...

He felt the nudge again, but then a voice spoke, a female voice.

"You have food here, eat before I am observed!"

He contemplated for a second, and then turned to see who spoke to him. He rubbed his eyes while he tried to focus into the voice.

Chee saw food in her cupped hands, and then slowly buried his face into them.

All the time he ate, he watched the form above him in the darkness of the hut, his eye's now darted and flitted around the sleeping hut, there was no other movement, but for these two.

Only pieces of mixed, hard dried food and some slices of raw vegetables, but he had never tasted nor savoured anything as welcome.

Not even in the great white box of magical flavours and new tastes.

He touched her cupped hands and gently held her fingers.

He ate the last of the food, licking every tiny crumb

from the lines of her palm and fingers. He held her hands and felt emotion beyond description; an enormous weight seemed lifted from him as someone showed care and compassion to him for the first time in this new and very strange family.

He cried into them, speaking lowly into her fingers.

"Thank you for showing me this kindness, you have no idea what your act means to me in this place"

He watched her silhouetted shape in the dimness of the hut while she replied.

"I had to help, to do something, you have went through so much, as Chian did"

He nodded unknowingly.

"Who was... Chian?"

"Chian was taken a time ago at Bowers hands, I thought and hoped so much"...

Then she started to weep softly.

"No, don't cry"

He could see her body begin to shake with emotion, she lifted a hand and covered her eyes.

"I watched them bring in with the hard house and hoped so much it was my older brother, Chian, brought home and recovered"...

Then Chee understood it was him and not her brother.

He continued to hold her hand.

"I'm sorry about Chian, if ever I can do anything to help your great sorrow over the loss of your brother"...

A motor vehicle rumbled past and she withdrew quickly from him.

"Female!" he gasped.

She turned, as she was about to exit the hut.

"What do I call you?"

He could see her turn at the door, and then she returned his gaze for a few moments.

In the dim light of the approaching night, the female who had fed him, the same one from two days since.

Watching him.

"Sareen"

He watched her exit the door, and then looked to the resting macaques around him.

Again, undisturbed.

He lay back down to consider her mercy.

She must think something of him, for her actions could cost her, and may still yet. He settled down and his last thoughts on it were to remind himself of her eyes, her beautiful brown, monkey eyes.

And the softness of her hands that he had eaten from.

Hours or moments had passed, the air around him seemed heavy and oppressing in the now virtual darkness, he turned dolefully from his resting position when a voice became apparent to him, soft, yet carrying through the gloom of the sleeping hut.

"Chee, awaken and turn to me"

He immediately became aware, he recognized the voice!

He screwed his sight and watched a soft glowing, beginning to appear before him.

Standing, almost floating before him, he watched incredulously as a figure became clearer through the still whiteness in the darkened hut.

He looked quickly around the sleeping troop, yet no one seemed disturbed by the white light.

And the figure growing inside it.

All slept on.

He attempted to swallow, and drew his lips across his tongue in complete astonishment.

Then he spoke lowly to the apparition before him.

"Mother?"

"Yes"

"Mother, is it you?" he gasped, unbelievingly.

She smiled serenely, and the year-old macaque felt himself rise, tear-filled to greet her.

He cried at the foot of the soft-light, wanting to know why she and the family had left him here, to this miserable existence of an unwelcome intruder in his own enclosure.

"Chee, from where we came is long and past, but rest tonight, you are home, this place where you are now, shall become great and good again, but at your hands"

"How Mother?"

"It can only be your doing; you have honorable work and many burdenous tasks to perform, some which you will think impossible, but with help, you can succeed!"

"I can?"

She nodded down to him, caressing his head as he lay at her feet, asleep, yet mindfully aware of the message from her to him.

"Only you will change the ways, and in time you will receive help, from those as yet unknown and unexpected!"

He nodded and shook his head incredulously as she spoke.

"Sleep on son, and I promise you in time, we will meet again"

Chapter 38

Things Change.

He awakened from the deepest sleep he could remember, just as the sun had started to creep over the trees surrounding the park.

He had never been so unsure, yet so doggedly aware of anything in his life, the message from his Mother was clear in his mind, there was much to do.

Much work, he had great faith in the happenings of last night.

The visit from his Mother, the vision in his subconscious, told him he would receive unexpected help.

Sareen.

He had started to receive that help already, he stood and made for the exit.

"Intruder sit down, you put me from my food!"

A younger macaque sitting close to him, as usual starting Chee's day with a grumble.

He leaned down and held the younger simians mouth closed with one hand.

"Be quiet Berra, and remain respectful when your elders pass"

The younger monkey watched on unbelievingly through wide, staring eyes to other males and females in the hut.

Chee then gripped his hand over the little ones head, encompassing it completely.

"And if you are lucky" he squeezed the youngsters skull firmly, "if you are very lucky, you may live long enough to become one!"

He picked a half-apple from the food pile and walked off out of the hut.

The child monkey could only watch on open-jawed, and for the first time since the intruders arrival, silently, as were the others.

He sat on the outskirts of the macaque enclosure and noted.

Bower stayed indoors most of the time, maybe this cool climate wasn't to his liking.

Chee viewed the area, took note of those that may be dangerous to him, and others who may be allied to him in time. Bowers two side-kicks were both roughly the same age, but slightly smaller than him. They didn't seem to have much about them and were both fawning and quite weak-minded. He figured he could take them both out, and probably even at the same time.

He had lived rough outside the camp for six months, a fair amount in his young lifetime. He had fought and scrapped with foxes, dogs and cats in the forest, he'd also been shot with a tranquillizing dart, stared the mad-dog in the eyes and survived, and had even came through the ordeal of the mass chase and terrible electrocution in the station, not that he remembered much of it though, if anything...

But all of his experiences on the other side of the fences, combined to make him one tough and shrewd cookie of a macaque, very resourceful, and quite able to fend and live by himself.

If he could survive the chase through the mall by the gun firing humans, he could look after himself here, he knew that, and also, his Mother had told him in the dream.

An older male macaque, to him a Koth, wandered

close and sat ten feet off him. He recognized it from his hut, another of low esteem. He nodded to the older simian, and smiled flashing confident teeth for the first time since his arrival, when the elder nodded back in assent.

"Who are you?"

"I'm a Chee monkey, and you?"

"Bodan"

They both nodded and flashed teeth, each watching around themselves for signs of Bower or his cronies. Chee touched his head with his hand, then held it open and dropped it down to his side.

The other macaque looked on in confusion.

"What?"

"It's a greeting", he explained, "It's what we do here!"

Bodan looked around the almost deserted enclosure and looked back sardonically.

"Greeting?" he smiled in irony.

They both watched some activity on the other side of the enclosure; three females exited the lead hut occupied by Bower and his allies. Two walked on but the other looked to the side where Chee and Bodan

sat and spoke.

Sareen.

He thought out loud, "She's a beautiful Chee; I feel my heart beat fast when she comes by"

Chee lifted an arm and waved, but she looked to ignore him. She sidled over to where a child monkey sat, and began to groom him, standing over his head.

Both macaques spoke quietly for some moments, watching her intently from a few metres off.

She spoke aloud, still inspecting the young macaque's

fur.

"I can't be seen to speak with you intruder, you have no esteem!"...

He spoke evenly in return.

"Chee"...

She stopped her search momentarily, and then looked over.

"That's my esteem; I'm a Chee working male!"

Slightly confused, she stopped picking, nipping and biting for a second.

"Where do you work, from here?" she asked quietly.

The child monkey went to stand up and leave, but was hauled down again and forced to remain, quite irked.

"Not finished Tori"...

She looked across and lifted her eyebrows for him to continue, and just then, just at that split second of her flash of eyes, Chee realized there was something about this female that held his attention longer than any he had ever known.

Again, he felt his inside's beat faster when they spoke.

He answered smiling toward her and the restless, resentful infant macaque.

"Not now, but before your new family arrived, the last family here was ruled by my Mother, the Maya, and we all worked"

Both Bodan and Sareen looked up to him.

He smiled a little and she screwed her face at the thought.

"Your Mother, was the lead macaque?"

He nodded in affirmation to Sareen, "Yes, just like you would be here, if I had my way"

By now she had stopped preening for some moments,

and had hardly noticed the child tiring and slipping away from her.

She remained in position, hands held at the height of the missing beast, and looked over to the new arrival.

"Me? Lead macaque?"

He nodded over quite positively while Bodan smiled wildly.

"What a macaque!" he whispered under his breath, just as the Chee monkey continued.

Now he stared a little sullenly toward the lead hut.

"The family should never be ruled with power and aggression, as he does, you should lead with wisdom and reason"

Sareen found herself thinking over what the intruder, Chee as he called himself, had said to her. He actually seemed to be independent-minded and nothing much like what the others had thought.

Weak-willed, servile, or ugly.

And there was actually something about his smile that she found she had quite liked, even if he did speak peculiarly, and come out with some quite odd statements, his Mother, the Maya? Whatever that was.

And herself, the lead macaque?...

She smiled at the thought of it anyway, and carried on with her day, wondering when she would next bump into him.

Chee's acquaintance with Bodan had led to clandestine introductions, meetings with Redo and Kaar, two other males of low-stock, only this time they were more of his age.

He told the three monkeys of his escape from the

park, of his time outside the fences, and of life with the humans, in the forest and of his journey to try and find home. He began to explain the legend of home to them. By now they weren't quite sure if he was the bravest macaque they had ever encountered, or if he was just, quite mad?

Chee had showed them the scars on his hands and arms, the grazing wound where the bullet had nicked into him. He didn't know what it was, but could only describe the intense, searing pain; it was like nothing else he had ever felt.

They could see for themselves the clumps and patches of missing fur on his body, some of it only now just starting to grow in again, while some never would. He seemed humorous and laughed at his own failings, as he explained the time with the mad-dog and the red squeaky ball, then he could be wonderfully wise with his learning's of life outside, how he survived the massive chase by the humans, and then the electrocution...

At times he could become sad and reflective, speaking of the former colony of working macaques, in his queer tongue, of Harree and the roll-houses, whatever they were, and the roles that the beasts had played in the many days since the new arrivals had come.

Still none of them were too sure of what he was.

Genuine?

Or sad, mad and completely?

Away with it...

Slowly, the stories of the intruder began to spread around the enclosure, of Chee, and his remarkable tales, and eventually word of it came to the lead hut, where Bower listened intently.

As yet there were no cars, or roll-houses, in the enclosure, but they were to be allowed to enter the enclosures soon, when the keepers considered the macaques had settled.

So Chee's stories of the past could never be backed-up with proof.

By now, almost one week after his first appearance, there was such a change in the demeanour of the new arrival, and the family's reaction to him. Warm and humorous with the adults, and because of the now near legendary stories of his exploits, the younger, inexperienced macaques approached him with a mixture of curious, yet cautious admiration, and by now, diminishing bravado. He now seemed confident and relaxed, now actually smiling along with the group.

There were fifteen macaques in the hut, of differing age and sex. Chee tried to show some of the others how to count.

"You hold your fingers here like this", he held both hands open, showing the ten digits, "That's how many are here in this room!"

Adults and children looked around themselves and smiled, then physically counted the ten with each digit of their hands.

They realized he was right, two hands!

"Over here, there is only this hand", he pointed to five individuals, then held his hand, closed in the other, "You see? This hand!"

They smiled amongst themselves; again he was right, the intruder, Chee, was right!

And then a voice thundered through the hut.

"Zymba, Tiyell, Sareen!"

Immediately, the conversation stopped.

Everyone turned in shock, and looked at Bower, straddling the doorway.

Sidekicks at either side of him.

"Why are you in this hut of low esteem?"

Two of the females looked ashamedly downward, while Sareen looked from the doorway to Chee in uncertainty.

Staring between them, Bower continued "I will speak with you after I have dealt with the intruder"

But the air was broken further, when another voice spoke out.

"I think your time for speaking to the families as you do is coming to its end".....

The tone was firm, clear and dispassionate.

And came from the intruder...

Bower glared from his position toward the other, seated with his back to him.

He watched him rise, and slowly, turn to face him.

The lead macaque glowered; his hateful eyes drew across the bodies in the hut, to the new arrival.

"YOUR EYE'S INTRUDER, WHAT DID I SAY OF YOUR EYE'S! WHAT DO YOU THINK YOU DO!"

Chee kept looking on, and then smiled over, quite charmingly, given the situation.

"I think you have forest-pig poo for brains!"...

Eyes around the hut opened wide in amazement and some even in suppressed mirth at the answer to the lead macaque! The two cronies standing by Bowers side were also visibly shocked!

They smiled anyway at the stupidity shown, now only one thing was going to happen and they coyly grinned in

Bowers direction.

The great macaque inhaled fully while he contemplated, drilling his eyes in the intruders form.

Then all in the room sat stone-faced as Bower answered, in his low and extreme rasp.

"You were not here when the last one was shown how we deal with those who question the way, so you will have to learn... personally!"

He looked in great confidence toward each of his cohorts, and then finished the warning, with chillingly cold smiles from the three.

"And... Painfully!"......

But just as Bower and the others stepped forward, they noticed movement on the far side of the hut.

Sareen stood up and sidled forward, watching the three lead male macaques.

Eye to eye.

Bower smiled to the others at the apparent foolishness of it, and leered in her direction.

He watched sullenly on as she walked over and stood at the side of the intruder.

Bower responded.

"Not you too, weak female? Is this because of your brother, to answer me?...

Neither Chee, the intruder, nor Sareen answered.

"You desire to learn the way also?"

Chee and Sareen stood resolutely, shoulder to shoulder.

Again the three lead macaques turned and smiled, but with now fully-bared teeth, glinting in the low sunlight.

This would make it more interesting, Bower considered, female macaques can be feisty defenders, and after he has consigned the intruder to his fate?

She would be his...

Again the three macaques went to walk toward them.

"Are you a fool?" asked Bower, in slow, savage tones, "You must know this is madness, my others will hold him, as I pull his stomach out"...

The lead macaque stood forward and inhaled deeply, intoxicated with his own reputation, then he paused.

Redo stood up and walked to Chee's side, and then Kaar followed.

Bower raised an eyebrow in confidant thought.

Then Bodan stood; now there were five...

The large Macaque raised his head and roared terribly into the air of the hut, the reverberation seemed to shake the hut to its foundations, and every macaque present.

Then he stood forward..

He looked down to the ground ahead of Chee, then nodded toward him, in invitation.

His opponent stepped forward, opening and closing his fingers in anticipation.

The two approached, and sidled around slowly, both eyeing each other hatefully.

As everyone expected, Bower flew forward, but in a flash, Chee slipped aside and quickly turned to follow the bigger macaque as he fell to the ground. As this happened, Kaar and Redo bolted in the direction of the other two and the room turned instantly into bedlam, as two clans fought for dominance in the confines of the hut. Chee and Bower took centre-stage, clawing, biting, and wrestling on the floor. Blood-soaked lumps of fur flew in all directions in the scream-filled hut. Sareen fought bravely against another female, and others who reckoned in the pre-ceding days that the intruder would be a better, fairer leader, clashed with the allies of Bower. The main battle continued, and Bower was slowly discovering to his dismay, that the intruder was a strong fighter.

After a brief but hectic spell of fighting, they paused and stood off each other, while both caught their breath.

All the others copied, standing as still as the two main battlers, flitting their untrusting vision from their opponents to the two would be leaders.

Bower looked over, still smiling confidently.

"Your end will be soon!"

Chee smiled in return, looking down to his bloodied hand.

He held it forward, showing the heavy blood-stains.

"This is your blood Bower, and it will become worse"...

Bowers eyes flared in realization, he looked down to a wound on his leg and raged internally.

He raced forward, still heaving for breath as the other simian again accepted the challenge. Battle resumed in the hut and now even the younger simians fought and bled,

Macaques clashed together all around the hut with some racing in from outside to join the affray, from both sides, but soon the fighting was taking its toll, so much so, the two macaques that had been allied to Bower were bolting out from the hut. Others were beginning to see the turning of the tide and slowly the fighting was lessening, Bowers sympathizers were now becoming weary and thinning, and eventually the only battle remaining was the grim duel between the two great macaques.

They rolled and fought, with each of them being dominant at varying times, but Bower was beginning to tire, and to his utter and growing disbelief, he could hardly see a weakness in his opponent.

Bower pushed the intruder away and stood aside, doubled up and heaving for breath.

As if to compound his situation, he then noticed none of his sympathizers were left in the hut.

He decided to gamble; now it was his last option.

He held out his open hand.

"Equal?"

The intruder stood erect, hands on hips, and to Bowers utter dismay, looking ready to continue.

"Equal?" repeated Bower.

Chee smiled, and then shook his head.

"You're beaten, you must submit!"

Bower looked around the hut.

Surrounded, not only by the opponent he knew he couldn't break, but also about a dozen others that stood close behind the other macaque.

The one that called himself Chee.

Now he knew all seemed lost, he smiled evenly as he agreed.

"Yes, I will submit"

He held out his paw in acceptance, and Chee stepped slowly forward in assent.

Then in a flash Bower seized the others paw and pulled him forward. He dived headfirst toward the other, forcing his jaws into the intruder's neck and searching feverishly to plunge his giant incisor teeth into the others jugular vein. The rest watched in shock as Bower continued the attack with seemingly renewed vigour. Both arms were wrapped powerfully around his opponent, enveloping him as a giant constrictor, but now his legs also tightened firmly around the others. Chee was almost helpless by this time, Bower had him enclosed completely, and his bared teeth were buried into his opponent's neck as he snapped and gnawed incessantly, trying to locate the main artery. But now Chee was tiring, he felt his strength deplete and the longer the larger Macaque continued the attack, the weaker he became. Bower tasted blood in his mouth and this invigorated him further, it flashed through his mind, now this was just a matter of time. This imposter to his throne, this would-be thief of his kingdom, will soon be dead.

Bower felt re-energized!

Galvanized!

He now felt the strength of ten macaque's course through his system, now was time for the kill. He was going to pull out this pretender's stomach, his intestines, and then lastly, his heart!!

AND THEN EAT THEM!!!!!

But without warning, with hardly any sense of feeling or sensation, Bower felt his opponent slip, and then felt a great force on his body.

He was catapulted at least ten feet high, none of the others could believe what they were watching as the larger macaque soared in the air of the hut and then landed with a sickening thud, in the collection of gnarled branches that the younger simians use to exercise.

Then there was silence...

They looked from Bower, who lay silent and horribly distended on the collection of wooden limbs, and then to Chee, who had performed the miraculous escape!

Sareen moved quickly to comfort Chee, and to help staunch the flow of blood which trickled from various neck wounds.

But thankfully, not from his main artery.

"How are you?" she asked.

Chee nodded without speaking, clutching his neck while slowly climbing from the floor, only watching Bowers still and unmoving body as he moved.

Then everyone followed as he slowly paced to where his opponent lay.

Standing over him, he nudged Bowers leg carefully.

Nothing, no movement, only wide-open, staring, but unseeing, eyes.

Sareen whispered.

"You have done it, Chee, you have done it!"...

Chapter 39

A Dish Best Served Cold, or Chilled…

"Okay, let's all check"

In the dull half-light of the cavern, George Dunbar looked to his older brother, sister-in-law, and then, his wife.

Jill.

"Right, got your torches?"

They all assented.

Except Jill

"Jill, you got yours?"

She nodded, expressionless.

George returned the nod, but with a smirk growing.

"Walkie-talkies?"

The other two nodded, but again, his wife demurred.

"Jill"

She held it up without speaking, again, stone-faced.

Once more, George looked on, his face still embellished with a very satisfied expression,

"Good" he stated, returning his happy gaze to the others.

"We've all got our ropes?"

Once more, his brother and sister in-law responded by holding onto ropes gathered around their shoulders and waist, smiling broadly.

But, nothing from Jill…

She had the rope.

Had the walkie-talkie.

And had the torch…

She just had no interest in what they were about to do.

To abseil 300 feet down into the dark and distant

bowels of earths inner core.

In more or less, complete bloody darkness.

She had no idea of what lived down there, anything, everything, with 2, 4, 6, 8 or even more legs!!

With pincers, PINCERS!!!

AND THEY CAN ALL SEE IN THE DARK!!!

She shivered once more at the thought..

She was convinced she was tunnelling downward, straight into Hell....

Do not pass go.

Do not pick up £200.

Go directly to.

Hell...

Jill couldn't imagine anything worse, she couldn't dream of anything she would rather not do.

She would prefer to have a tooth-pulled.

Without the anaesthetic.

Have her head shaved, or plucked...

Gladly.

Electric-shock treatment

Or eat a bush-tucker trial...

But sadly, these luxuries were not an option.

Because, she had promised George.

Jill inhaled deeply with the memory, shaking her head as she remembered her own words.

"If you can just prove that there is a monkey George..."

Chapter 40

Everything Changes, but somehow…

Once again, Harry Ramsay smiled through what seemed like a twelve-inch grin as he looked down.

He could hardly believe what was sitting there in front of him; he shook his head, grinning awfully at the sight of it.

This was now three months later and everything seemed to have settled, quite nicely, thank you very much, in the new monkey's quarters.

Sure, there had been a period of time when various males had fought for dominance; so much so, two of them had been killed.

This again he knew was nature's way, this type of thing happened continually in the wild, and in confinement, as the safari park.

But this he could see, there was now harmony, stability had returned, and there was an order and purpose to the clan of macaque's day.

Fantastic!

He turned from the objects in front of him and smiled to the family of monkeys.

And what sat between them.

A number plate!

A wheel trim!!

And a windscreen wiper blade!!!

All, in offer to him!!!

He now knew that Tawny, (or Sonny, or Squeaky, or Chee) had brought about this incredible change, and he was now almost dumbfounded by its implications.

"Hello there" he said softly, not realizing, that the macaque's journey had turned full-fold.

Chee had sought to find the legendary fabled-land of home, but sadly, hadn't landed in the heat-seared plains of India, nor the sub-tropical climates of China, or Japan.

Or even sun-kissed Gibraltar

He hadn't discovered the old land that his Mother, and hers, had lauded of.

But had come...

"Well done Tawny" he said, with no idea of the irony in his words.

"Welcome home"...

The End

Afterword

In April 2000, 89 Rhesus Macaques were culled upon the terrible discovery of an outbreak of Simian Herpes B. virus at Blair Drummond Safari Park in Scotland. This disease is potentially fatal to humans, a young girl in America had recently died after a monkey had spat at her, so a hard decision was made and the animals were humanely shot.

Also, in England, Woburn Safari Park and West Midlands Safari and Leisure Park, killed 245 monkeys between them.

This was an utter disaster, friends I spoke to felt shocked by the news which was carried by the National media, everyone who had experience of them smiled fondly and sadly with their memories…

I had actually started writing the story after a visit to Blair Drummond with my Wife, Dianne, and daughter Angela. The macaques charmed each of us perfectly; so much so, Angie wanted to take one home that had been clambering about our car. I was well into the opening chapters when the news broke, we all mourned a little and I had named and characterised many of the little simians, and then?

I have to say, I was in total personal shock with the awful news.

It took me about a week, but eventually, a Eureka

moment occurred...

I used this sad piece of history and included it in my story of Chee, and the rest, as they say.

Is His Story...

I was delighted to learn that, in 2015, Blair Drummond had decided to reintroduce a clan of Rhesus Macaque monkeys. I could hardly believe how fact had followed fiction, (well in my story anyway) and the macaques were rehomed with new quarters, as in Esc-Ape!

They were brought from the Island of Gibraltar where they had virtually outgrown their neighbourhood. A cull of 30 of the simians of the Rock had been contemplated, but thankfully a transfer to Scotland was chosen instead.

The Macaques must have enjoyed the fantastic Southern Spanish climate, warm weather from morning till night. They're probably now all wondering where the sun has gone, it's just a bit cooler here and that's putting it mildly.

Never the less, the monkeys are now establishing themselves, and are becoming many peoples highlight in the Park, and I am a little happier in life with their reintroduction.

Welcome Home.

Esc-Ape!

Alan Milligan

Also by Alan Milligan

Michael: The Discarnate Soul
Tommy Two-Pieces: Sentient
The Millennium Gate: A Tale of Regression

Printed in Great Britain
by Amazon